The Right Family

Susan B. Roara

Printed in the United States of America
Edited by Kristen Corrects, Inc.

First edition published 2015
10 9 8 7 6 5 4 3 2 1

B. Roara, Susan
The right family / Susan B. Roara
p. cm.
ISBN-13: 978-0-9967822-1-0
ISBN-10: 0-9967822-1-4

Table of Contents

CHAPTER 1

Lucy

There was a look she got when she lost control of her actions. I've seen it many times, that angry look. It began with her eyes. It started with her inability to look you in your face, for fear that her emotions would become known to you and to the others. The feelings of hatred, disappointment, and frustration shoved deep down inside her, yet visible all over her expression in that awkward, frowned appearance that made her look ugly all over.

Then there was the voice.

The changes to her voice that clearly indicated and warned you that something bad was about to happen. It started with a little ranting. The underlying mumbling you heard, that this was all your fault. If it weren't for you, life would have been perfect. You're the reason why she acted this way. You did this.

And then it began. The screaming. The high-pitched release of sound and dissatisfaction that exploded out of her mouth, rendering her victims shocked and confused. Everything she'd bottled up vomiting in your presence. The violent attack of words and actions that left you battered and assaulted physically, shaken and disoriented mentally, as to how could I make this better. How could I fix this?

Then there were the faces.

The horrified look of terror and fear on all the little people's faces, haunting you. The children who had been unwillingly sucked out of their warm, comfortable beds to witness the breakdown of their loved one, left horrified and crushed, tears streaking down their cheeks. The heartbreaking sense that one person was sucking the innocent souls right out of the room, forever changing them.

Then coffee and donuts. Laughter ensued and everything was right again. Things appeared normal and life began to move. You forgave and continued on. But you never forgot. The ugliness was bound to rear its head once again, and you silently waited for it and watched for the signs.

That was my mother.

Despite her faults and her uneasy ways, the world was a far better place with her in it. As all young children think, I thought she would be mine forever. I never thought anything bad would ever happen to my mother.

I was wrong.

CHAPTER 2

Lucy

I could hear my sister Julia screaming at my mother. Complaining to her that she couldn't find her brand new shirt that she bought. I could imagine that my mother was rolling her eyes at her, trying to distract her with simple statements like, "Maybe it's in the laundry, Julia. Perhaps you left it at a friend's house?"

My heart was pounding, for I knew I didn't have much time. I began running frantically from my room to hers in an effort to hide the shirt. I knew that she would suspect me of taking it. How could I not take the shirt? I *loved* that shirt. I thought it was the coolest shirt I had ever seen. I didn't get to wear nice clothing like Julia. Julia was in high school and she was able to work and buy her own clothes. The only thing that I was able to wear was the hand-me-down items from my sister Kathryn and from my mother's neighborhood girlfriends, whose children had grown. Worn clothes with stains and small tears in them that my mother attempted to fix and reuse over and over again. I appreciated her efforts, but *come on!*

I tried so carefully to fold Julia's shirt as if it had never been touched before and then I frantically shoved the thing into her dresser drawer. I could hear her pounding up the wooden stairs, every loud step she took sending darts of fear into my chest.

We lived in a Cape Cod home in a small town in Connecticut. I lived with my parents and six of my siblings. Ours was a typical small town, full of working class families trying to make ends meet, living off one working income. Neighborhoods were tight with small houses. Large families stuck together, neighbors helped one another. Small brick businesses and buildings lined our town center and everyone worked at the steel factory. Water wheels produced energy then and people were conscious of how they lived. You felt safe when you walked down the streets; you felt a part of the community. I didn't feel safe now; now I felt trapped.

I had to make it across the hall before she saw me. Her room was opposite mine, a quick five feet of hallway space separating them. There were only two bedrooms on the second floor so there was nowhere else to run. I slammed the dresser drawer shut and ran. I ran across the hall, my heart exploding out of my chest as if Jason—that scary guy who killed people in that movie that my mother wouldn't even consider to let me watch—were chasing me. I flew on top of my bed and grabbed my school-required reading book and pretended to be busy, pretended to read the words that were on the page but I could barely see straight, let alone concentrate.

Julia opened my door with extreme force, as if the door weighed a hundred pounds. "Lucy?!" she hollered, her eyes narrowing in on my guilt-ridden face.

"What's the matter, Julia? I can hear you yelling all the way up here," I asked, hoping my voice didn't quiver quite as much as my heart did.

"Where is my shirt? I know you took it," Julia accused with her hands on her hips, her lips pursed.

"Did you check the laundry, Julia? Perhaps it's there; maybe Mom hasn't gotten to it yet. Do you want me to check for you?" I stood from my bed and walked around her, trying eagerly to escape. The laundry was no place for a child, but I was willing to pretend to look down there to get away from her. The laundry room was located in the dark and dreary basement of our home. I hated the basement. The mountain of clothing that we created by tossing laundry carelessly down the flight of stairs and onto the cellar floor was overwhelming. Some articles of clothing never quite made it to the concrete flooring below but was instead scattered carelessly along the edges of the stairway. Don't forget the creepy, dark corners of the room

12

where the spiders lived. No, I didn't want to go into the basement, but I would. I needed to get away.

"I checked the laundry, it's not there," Julia spat, ignoring my suggestion as she continued to open my dresser drawers, pulling out my clothes and throwing them onto the floor.

"You're going to clean this, Julia! Mama works hard to do the laundry!"

Her abusive attitude was starting to irritate me. I began to gather my clothes and carefully folded them and placed them back into my drawers. "Why don't you leave, you're not helping anybody. You're just making a mess."

Julia sat on the floor next to me, defeated by her attempts to locate the shirt. She stood and moved toward the door. As she twisted the knob, she turned back and glanced at me. "I better not find out you have it," she warned, her voice calm and deliberate.

I watched her leave. I stood there and waited. I knew it was only a matter of minutes before all hell would break loose. Once Julia located her shirt, which was worn and possibly stained in the bottom corner, she was going to be beyond angry. I decided perhaps I should leave; maybe I should go to my friend Amelia's house and let Julia calm down a bit.

I walked toward the connecting hallway, but it was too late. Julia had already opened her bedroom door and was standing there, her face contorted in anger, her hands visibly shaking as she began to speak.

"You're such a little bitch! *I can't stand you!* All you do is lie." Tears welled in her eyes as she clutched onto the hairbrush she grasped tightly, her white knuckles visible as she spat her hateful words at me.

"I'm sorry, Julia," I said with a small smile on my face. I didn't mean to smile, but when I'm nervous, I tend to laugh. It's a horrible problem.

Julia lunged at me with ease as she blocked the only escape route I had to the ground floor. There was nowhere to go but backward. As I tried to back into my bedroom, Julia took her hairbrush and smacked me with it, smashing it hard across the bridge of my nose. Shocked by her assault, I noticed the blood dripping down my face, escaping from my nostrils and across the back of my hand as I wiped it clean.

"You deserve it!" she screamed in my face. "You deserve everything you get!" She turned and retreated to her bedroom, leaving me standing there, shaken and fuming. I took one look into the mirror and carefully inspected the damage on my face. *Oh god, what will my friends say? What will my teachers think?*

I grabbed a fistful of tissues and ran down the stairs to the bottom floor. I ran past my mother as she was cooking dinner. I could hear her singing softly to herself, "I fall to pieces..."

She stopped and looked at me as I hurried past her. "Lucy, are you alright?"

I didn't stop to respond. I continued to whisk through the dining room and out the front door. I ran down the driveway, passing through the scattered toys, bikes, and tricycles in our front yard and down the street past all my neighbors' houses. Homes that were built exactly like ours, small homes that looked exactly the same, one right after another, lining our small neighborhood street. Large oak trees offered shade on every corner of every property. I ran past my friend Jack's house and I could see him standing there mowing his lawn, staring at me as I kept running.

"Lucy!" he screamed, but I couldn't stop.

I ran up the battered driveway of the fish and game club, the asphalt coming apart at the entrance, the broken gate unlocked and hanging with its rusted ends touching the ground. I ran down the marked hiking paths full of rough tree roots and small boulders. The biking trails were suitable only for a mountain bike, tripping me as I ran toward the waterfalls at the other end of the pond. There was nowhere to go once I reached the waterfall, so I stopped. I fought back my tears and forcibly made myself sit and take deep breaths. I glanced around myself and at the waterfalls. Everything was green and lush, the rocks covering the small stream, slippery and full of moss. The trickling sounds of water flowing from the waterfall were tranquil and peaceful. I could hear my heart rate calming, my breathing becoming steadier, and my anxiety subsiding. I thought about Julia. She had so much anger over a little shirt. How does she get to that point of frustration?

I closed my eyes and listened to the woods that surrounded me. I put my head between my legs and rested as I listened to the insects chirping, the crickets and the bullfrogs, fighting to be heard. I could hear the birds gawking from up above me in the trees, as if to say, "We see you Lucy; we know what just happened." I reached up and touched my nose, flinching from the pain as I felt the tackiness of the blood starting to dry.

As I sat, I thought about my story. Perhaps I fell off a bike or maybe I tripped and scraped my face on the sidewalk. As much as I disliked Julia at times, I didn't want people to think she was a horrible monster. It was humiliating, to have to explain this fight we had.

Suddenly, I heard twigs breaking and the rustling of footsteps through the leaves behind me. I quickly turned to look and it was Jack. He stood there, staring at me, his eyes full of concern. I turned back around, embarrassed, not wanting him to see me this way. Not wanting to cry in front of him. He was my friend. But, he was more than that.

He stood beside me, and then slowly sat down next to me on the large boulder nestled in front of the waterfalls. He looked over into my face and I could hear him take a deep breath, one of frustration and irritation. He grabbed my hand and held it tight. He spoke no words of comfort, no words of hatred toward my abuser; he just sat there, quiet and still. I wanted desperately to cry. If I spoke my words, the tears would have released themselves and it would have been all over.

Instead, we sat holding hands.

And it was perfect.

CHAPTER 3

Lucy

The next morning I lay in bed and waited for Julia and Thomas to finish using the bathroom. Getting ready for school in the morning always posed challenges at my house, being that we had the one shower. The single bathroom was off limits until my older siblings were done using it. They started school much earlier than my younger siblings and I. They were in high school, I was in middle school, and my younger siblings were in elementary school.

Julia casually opened the door into my bedroom and stared at me from the entranceway. She looked like she was feeling some sort of remorse but, then again…not really. She tried to apologize in her snotty *don't touch my things* sort of way. I wasn't very interested in making up. I rolled away from her and faced the other direction, refusing to respond, and that was the end of it.

I dreaded going to school that day. I tried to lay in bed for as long as I could. I tried to fake illness but my mother wasn't having any part of it.

I got ready and dressed as slow and leisurely as possible. Deliberately trying to be late. My hair was long and snarled. I tried to tame it, brushing it smoothly. I surrendered and decided to braid my hair instead, hoping to gain some control over it. My younger sisters Kaylan and Jessica yelled for me. They couldn't do anything on their own.

"Lucy, do these shoes match?" Kaylan asked.

"They do match, Kaylan, but I think it's a little chilly outside for sandals. How about a pair of sneakers?" I suggested.

"I can't tie my shoes!"

"I can tie them for you."

"Okay," she replied in her husky, sleepy morning voice.

"Jessica? You need to get dressed before Mom starts to yell," I hollered across the room. My younger sisters and I shared a bedroom, while my older sisters Julia and Kathryn shared the room across the hall. Kathryn was my favorite sister. She graduated high school and although she still lived here with us, she was never home. She would have been really upset with Julia, had she been here. Kathryn was easygoing; she would

19

have never reacted physically toward me if I had borrowed her shirt. She would have been happy to share it. She was the best.

"I can't find anything to wear!" Jessica screamed as she stomped her feet.

"Get a life," I said. "You have tons of clothes, now hurry up. I'm going downstairs in five minutes so if you need my help, you need to hurry." The threat of me leaving always seemed to motivate them. Jessica had her sneakers on in no time and Kaylan was able to find suitable clothing. As I helped Kaylan zip her sweatshirt, she looked into my face.

"I hate her," she murmured.

"Who?" I asked.

"Julia!"

"Don't hate Julia."

"She's mean."

"It's okay, Kaylan. It was my fault too. I shouldn't have worn her shirt."

"Your nose looks sore." Kaylan tried to reach up and touch it.

Ugh, I thought. Everyone was going to notice my nose today. What would I say, how would I explain it? I gave Kaylan a little hug and told her not to worry about me. "Let's go eat some breakfast."

Mom had cereal out on the table for us. I grabbed a bowl and sat in front of the TV. "You need to hurry, Lucy. I don't want you late for school," Mama said. I rolled my eyes, dragged myself out of the chair, and picked up my backpack. Mama was sitting at the table in her fluffy bathrobe and worn-to-shreds slippers, having a conversation with Mikey, my youngest brother. The eight-year-old was a dark-haired, blue-eyed ball of energy. I would have bent down to kiss him, but he was eating pancakes with his fingers instead of a fork. That's all I needed was to smell like syrup before I got to class.

"Bye, Mom," I said, smiling at Mikey.

"Bye, Lucy. Try to have a good day, honey."

I leaned over the table and gave my mother a kiss. With my backpack on, I slowly turned and walked through the front door. I usually walked to school with Jack and I waited for him at the corner. I glanced down the street several times at his house, but he was nowhere in sight. It was about a ten-minute walk, mostly uphill. I could see some of my friends up ahead, but I was definitely late that morning, so I walked alone. I wish I had a little distraction. Being alone with my own thoughts was making me anxious. The lump in my throat was irritating me. I tried to put myself in my sister's shoes. I tried to understand her anger. Given the opportunity again, I probably

21

would have worn the shirt a second time. Had she pushed me or pulled my hair, I could have accepted this, no problem. Now I was embarrassed of the injury on my face and angered with her behavior over the shirt. What she did was unforgivable. I couldn't easily ignore it.

My breathing was deep and deliberate. I could feel anxiety running through my chest and arms as I approached my school. Deep breaths, deep breaths. I walked through the halls with my head down, avoiding as much eye contact with my classmates as possible. I walked into my classroom and sat in my school desk chair, thankful to finally get to class. No one noticed so far. My teacher, Mrs. A, asked us to line up for our next class. I went to stand in line with the others. Mrs. A was very pretty and she was always kind to me. She was my favorite teacher. She stood in the front of the line and counted our heads one by one. She stopped at me, bent down, and looked into my face. "Lucy! What happened to you?"

And there it was. I tried to stop it, but I couldn't. The lump in my throat wouldn't allow me to. My face crumbled and my eyes watered.

Don't cry…don't cry…

Crying.

CHAPTER 4

Lucy

Growing up in our neighborhood, the kids ruled. We spent hours playing Hide & Seek and Ghost in the Graveyard. Friends were always coming in and out of our house, staying for dinner and playing in our yard. My mother, of course, tried her best to please everyone. This task was very difficult with having a large family, but she attempted in many ways to be a good neighborhood mother.

Jack and I were inseparable. And who could forget about Charles, Jack's brother. Although he was older than us by several years, we did everything we could to be in his presence. We watched him work on his dirt bike for hours, we watched him play football in the streets with the older kids. We bothered him while he flirted with some of the neighborhood girls. We treated my brother Thomas the same way. Thomas was perfect: He was popular, strong and funny, and he was my favorite person to be with. Jack and I were always eager to please him. We were always flattered when he included us in something mischievous. Thomas and Charles were cool beyond belief, and everybody thought so.

Jack and Charles lived down the road at 177 Balsom Lane, in a white Cape Cod home with black shutters. Their mother, Donna, with wild red hair and big boobs, would open the door in her nightgown, smoking a cigarette with a glass of wine in her hand. She embarrassed those boys daily with her antics. I found her to be quite amusing at times, but, then again, she wasn't my mother.

Jack and Charles were independent and strong boys who made the neighborhood explode daily with entertainment and activity. Charles Nimchak was authoritative and intelligent. Jack, however, was the handsome one. It was difficult to stay angry with that boy, for his cuteness made me laugh and giggle. Charming, to say the least. Other boys followed closely behind as they led the neighborhood, while the girls and I stood by watching.

Donna Nimchak tried her best to raise the boys but the constant flow of men and alcohol drove her children away from her. Mr. Nimchak was rumored to have left his family years ago, before the boys reached their second birthday. I guess he had enough of her craziness. One thing was for sure:

There was little that Mrs. Nimchak could do to gain any respect from her sons. I think she gave up a long time ago.

Jack and I had big plans. Every day we had plans, but tonight felt like it was going to be special. I heard him knocking on my door as my mother answered and graciously invited him in.

"Lucy, honey? Jack's here!" Mama yelled up the stairs. Then, in a quieter voice, I heard her say, "Have a seat, Jack. She'll be down in a minute."

I could hear him downstairs talking with my mother and I could imagine that he was looking around shyly, feeling uncomfortable and nervous. I giggled to myself as I took my time in a slow effort to get ready, knowing Jack was being tortured by my mother's one hundred questions.

"Are you hungry, Jack?" my mother asked.

"No, we just had dinner. A bunch of kids and I are going to play Hide & Seek. I wanted to see if Lucy wanted to come."

"Sounds fun. I'm sure she would like that. Lucy! Are you coming?"

I walked down the stairs and grabbed my sweater. "Hey Jack," I said casually. Jack jumped up off his seat, happy to see me.

"Hey, Luce. Do you want to come hang with us?"

"Yeah, sure! Is that okay, Mom?"

"Yes, that's fine. Not too late, Lucy."

Jack and I said goodbye to my mother. We walked out of the front door, Jack quickly shoving me out of his way as he eagerly jumped off the three steps onto the driveway.

"Show off," I said, laughing.

"We're meeting a bunch of kids off Alan Street. It's just a quick walk. We'll be partners, you and I." Jack ran a little in front of me. He turned to walk backward so he could talk and look at me at the same time.

"I have the perfect hiding spot, Jack," I said. "In Mr. Johnson's small Christmas tree farm." Christmas tree farms were common in our town, along with the apple orchards and blueberry fields. Farm life in Connecticut was bountiful during the summer months and continued into fall where you could view the endless farm stands full of pumpkins and gourds. And then Christmas! Parking lots full of shoppers and lined with Christmas trees for sale, some full of twinkling lights and others wrapped tightly like a cocoon.

"I think I know where you're talking about. Everyone is using flashlights so we'll be able to sort of see each other. I brought you an extra one."

26

"Great! This is going to be fun!" I said, excitement bubbling up in my voice.

"Come on, Lucy. Let's hurry so we can catch up with everyone."

Jack grabbed my hand and we started to jog down the road until we reached Alan Street. I could see the flashlights flickering in the distance, like lightning bugs but bigger. We turned on our flashlights and quickly ducked into one of the Christmas trees. It was the perfect spot. Six large Christmas trees formed a circle with a big clearing in between. Jack and I crossed our legs and sat quietly. We could hear some of our friends yelling at each other in the distance.

"If someone yells your name, you're out of the game," Jack whispered to me.

"Who else is playing, so I know who to look for?"

"A bunch of people. Eddy and Tim are here somewhere, and I'm sure Alex and Anthony who live over on Bartlett Lane are here as well. I'm not sure who else."

Jack stared down into my face as he spoke quietly into the darkness. We turned off our flashlights and sat close together. Jack placed his arm around my waist and moved his face closer to mine. I could smell the fresh scent of bath soap on his skin; I noticed his freshly combed hair and the neatness of his overall appearance.

27

"Lucy, do you ever think about what it would be like if we kissed?" Jack asked carefully, his voice barely audible.

I'm glad that it was dark enough to hide the shocked expression on my face but I'm almost positive that Jack could hear my heart beating right out of my chest. *Of course I do! Of course I do!* My words escaped me as I stared at him, his lips coming closer to mine. He hesitated to wait for my response, but I gave none. He kissed me softly, a gentle kiss on my lips, sudden and perfect. I stared back at him after it was over, and smiled shyly. He pulled me closer to him and held his arm around me tight. I sat in silence as I thought about the kiss. I couldn't wait to tell my best girlfriend Amelia. She was going to die when she found out about this.

"JACK AND LUCY!"

"Dammit," Jack said. It was that little skinny James, creeping around the tree farm.

"You guys are out!" Jimmy said, pointing at us.

"Yeah yeah, we get it, we hear you," Jack said, annoyed. We both stood and brushed the pine needles off our pants.

"Come on, Lucy. Let's get out of here. It's getting late. I don't want your mom to be angry with me." Jack grabbed my hand again and we ran through the Christmas trees to the road.

"Let's take the shortcut to your house, Jack, and I'll go home from there," I suggested.

"You sure, Lucy?"

"Yeah, it's way quicker."

Jack continued to talk and walk backward.

I smiled at him. "You're going to hurt yourself, walking like that."

"Well, I don't want to be rude and I like to look at you when we talk."

"You're weird, Jack." I felt the flush of humid heat rise into my face as I laughed, embarrassed.

"So, what are you going to do this summer? Any plans?" Jack glanced shyly at me, awkwardly trying to fill the silence as we began to move on from our intimate moment, returning to the place where we were friends, just friends.

"Actually, my mother wants to send me to my grandmother's farm, up in Vermont. We're leaving in a few days."

"Oh, really?" Jack said. The disappointment was clear in his voice.

"Yes, it's a wonderful place. I'm looking forward to it. We'll be back. I'm sure it won't be all summer. What about you, Jack?"

"Oh, I'll probably be riding dirt bikes and swimming at the pool, maybe play some baseball, whatever I feel like."

"I love summer. I'm so happy school is out." I kicked a stone across the road.

We walked up the hill past a series of chrysanthemums and quickly approached Jack's house. There were several vehicles in the driveway. Jack looked at his house and said, "What a shithole" under his breath.

"What's that?" I asked, surprised by his attitude.

"Nothing. Looks like my mother has company is all."

I looked at Jack and I could feel his irritation about the situation. "Do you want to come home with me, Jack? I'm sure my mother would let us watch a movie."

Jack smiled at me. "I don't want your mother to think there's something wrong. She'll ask questions and then I'll have to lie to her. Watching a movie sounds great right about now, though. I wish I could."

"When will Charles be home?"

Jack shrugged. "Sometimes he doesn't come home at all. He spends a lot of time at Jimmy's house. His parents are never home." Jack smiled mischievously. "Come on, Lucy, let's go look in on my mother, see what's going on." Jack grabbed my arm and we ducked past the front of the house into the back. Jack was much taller than I. I stood on my tiptoes and he and I looked into the back window by the kitchen. I could see Jack's mother sitting on someone's lap. She was throwing her head back and laughing. Two other men were sitting at the table playing cards and another woman was in the kitchen making a drink. The music was blaring and the men were loud and obnoxious.

Jack sighed. "It'll be like this all night."

I stopped and looked at Jack. He seemed so sad, so alone.

"Come on, Lucy, I'll walk you home."

"What are you going to do, Jack?" I asked as he led me through the front yard.

"Don't worry about me, Lucy. I'll find some of the guys and we'll hang out for a while. I don't have a curfew, so I'll stay busy till my mother's friends leave."

"Why does she have to be like that?" I asked. My mother was crazy at times but I never felt uneasy. I always felt safe when I went home.

"I don't know. She's always been this way for as long as I could remember." Jack walked me to my front door. I looked into the window. My mother, Mikey, and Kaylan were snuggled on the couch, watching a movie. Everything was normal.

"Are you sure you won't come in?" I asked softly.

"I'll be fine, Lucy. Can you come see me in the morning, before you leave?"

I smiled, remembering that I was leaving soon and because Jack wanted to see me again. "I'll be there early!"

Jack turned and started running down the street. He spun around and yelled back at me, "You stink at Hide & Seek by the way."

I laughed. "So do you!"

CHAPTER 5

Lucy

It wouldn't have been the first time I woke Donna up early in the morning in my attempts to get Jack's attention. I just hoped she didn't open the door this time. It was difficult to get out of a conversation with her if she was drinking, and you never knew what to expect from her. Sometimes she was happy to see you, sometimes she was annoyed, and other times she would cry, emotional and weepy. If I woke her up, she was surely going to be annoyed with me, especially since she had her friends over last night. I was eager to see Jack and hoped for the best.

It was a quiet day in the neighborhood; I could feel the heat starting to rise and could tell it was going to be a hot day. A lot of the kids went to the town pool during the day to cool off. I half expected Jack and I would be doing the same thing today. My mother decided we would leave for Vermont the next morning; she needed an extra day to get ready and I needed to spend one more day with Jack. Thinking of him made me smile.

When I reached Jack's house, I noticed the front door was a little off center. One of the hinges must be loosening because the door was lopsided. The lawn needed mowing. Jack and Charles usually did those chores when they felt like it. There were no vehicles in the driveway. *Good*, I thought. Maybe Donna wasn't home after all. Maybe she finally went to work for a change.

I reached the front door and rang the doorbell. No one answered, but I swore I saw Jack move the curtain a little to peek through. I banged on the door.

"JACK!" I said. "Let me in. It's getting hot!" I waited a few minutes, rang the bell again. No answer. I started to turn around to leave. Finally, Jack started to crack open the door.

"What do you want, Lucy? I thought you were going to Vermont for the summer. Why are you here?" Jack stood in the doorway just partly, just enough to speak to me but not enough for me to see his face.

"Hey Jack!" I said. "My mother wants to leave tomorrow instead. Besides, you asked me to come before I left." I stared at Jack in shock at his attitude toward me. He's never been short or rude to me. I couldn't understand what his problem was. Jack stood there, staring at me, not really speaking but looking at me, sort of dazed. "My mother baked you cookies, Jack," I said as I lifted the plate to show him. Jack stood back and opened the door to let me in his house.

I walked through the front door and Jack shut it behind me. As he turned to look at me, I gasped at what I saw. "*Jack!* What happened to you?" I asked. Jack's eye had been blackened and there were small bandages just above his cheek. His lip was swollen and his right arm was wrapped and dressed—sprained, I guess. Jack reached for the plate of cookies, his hands visibly shaking.

"Jack, please, sit down for a minute. I will put these in the kitchen," I said.

I walked through the living room and into the kitchen. The countertops were cluttered with beer cans, wine bottles, and ashtrays. There were dishes everywhere, pots and pans soiled with leftover food. The garbage was overflowing…and the smell. It was awful. I stopped in my tracks, shocked at what I saw. Everything was overwhelming. I couldn't leave the cookies; there was nowhere to put them. I walked back into the living room where Jack sat with his head down, unable to look at me.

"Jack, I don't know what is happening here but you need help. My mother will help you." I stood and watched him, waiting for him to respond. He continued to look nervously at his hands. "What is happening?" I asked again.

Jack looked up finally. "Lucy, this is no place for you. I'm so embarrassed." He stood, angry and upset, his eyes watering. He tried to get around me.

I grabbed hold of his arm and asked, "Please, Jack, who did this to you? Where is your mother?"

"My mother is gone. I don't know where; she left last night. Her boyfriend and I got into it. They were drinking and loud. I couldn't take it anymore, Lucy. I should have kept my mouth shut. Charles has been a wild man, trying to find them." His eyes widened. "You can't tell your mother, Lucy. She'll call the police. They'll take Charles and me away. I'd have to move somewhere else. I don't want to. *Please, Lucy.* You can't tell. Promise me."

Jack had both his hands on my shoulders, his eyes full of fear. All I could do was hug him. So I hugged him and he cried. He cried for a long time. He was such a sweet boy. His hair a mess, his clothes a mess. His face, beautiful. His big eyes and his dimples, beautiful. His soul, beautiful. I let him cry. I felt so bad for him. What could I do?

Finally, he stepped back from our embrace. I looked up at him. "Jack, I promise I won't tell. Please, let me help you. I can clean for you. Okay, Jack?"

"Okay. Thank you," Jack said, exhausted. "I'm so sorry."

I grabbed his hand and sat him down in a chair. I handed him the plate of cookies, and he began to eat them. From the look of it, I didn't think he'd eaten in a week. I slowly started clearing the clutter of garbage and dishes and bottles of beer. Jack finished eating and then began to help me. We cleaned together, the entire house for hours. We didn't speak much, but our eyes met often, as we both understood each other. I showed him how to do laundry. I made his bed and looked into the refrigerator for food. Of course, there was none.

"Jack, what are you going to do?" I asked.

"I don't know, Lucy. I need a little time to think it through. Charles is old enough; he'll be able to work. We can figure it out. We can manage on our own. We're better off." I wasn't sure if he was trying to convince me or himself.

I shook my head; I couldn't believe that this was happening to them.

"Lucy please, you've done so much."

I looked at my watch. "I need to go home soon. My mother will start to notice I've been gone too long." I chuckled. "Or maybe she won't." I shrugged my shoulders in exaggeration. Jack smiled slightly, a little laugh.

"I think she notices when you're missing. She loves you so much." Jack walked me to the door. I felt like I'd helped. The mess had been cleaned. I promised Jack not to say anything to anyone, to give him time. I only agreed to this if he let me back tomorrow with some food for him and Charles.

"Jack, you have to do something. You need to tell Charles to mow the lawn. People will start to notice if everything falls apart. You need to keep it tidy," I told him.

Jack nodded curtly. "You're right. I'll tell Charles, if he ever comes back."

I stared at Jack, so worried for him, not wanting to leave him alone, but I knew my mother would come looking for me. I knew Jack didn't want her to know.

"Thank you, Lucy; you really are my best friend." His eyes, I will never forget. They looked right through me.

"I'll be back tomorrow," I said.

Jack bent down to give me a hug and a small kiss on my cheek. "Goodbye, Lucy."

"Bye, Jack. Take care tonight." I turned and walked up the sidewalk. Jack closed the door.

My heart, my heart felt so heavy. I walked up the road toward my house, trying to think of what I would tell my mother. Could I trust her? What would she do? My mind raced.

38

I stood as I watched a police car pull down our road. As the car pulled past me, I saw Charles in the backseat. His face looked fearful and angry. They drove by and pulled into the driveway of the Nimchak household.

I turned to run home. I needed to speak to my mother, quickly. What were they doing? What was happening? As I rushed to open the door to my house, my mother was standing, waiting for me.

"MOM! MOM! The police! Jack and Charles and something is happening!" I yelled, panic taking hold of me. "You need to help them!"

"Lucy," my mother stated calmly. "Please sit down, honey. I know what is happening, but I need to talk to you, so sit down, sweetheart."

I sat. I tried to catch my breath. I looked into my mother's eyes. Hers too were full of sadness and pity.

"Mom, what is it?"

"They found Mrs. Nimchak, Donna, this afternoon."

"They did!" I said, standing up. "Good! She can come home, then, with Jack and Charles!"

"No honey, she can't," Mom murmured. "She died, Lucy. Mrs. Nimchak has died."

"What?" Tears started to fill my eyes and I couldn't seem to catch my breath. I felt scared, sad, nervous. "What will happen to Jack and Charles?"

"I don't know, honey, but I promise you, I will do everything I can to help them boys. You know I will, Lucy." She bent down to hug me.

"Mom, Jack has bruises all over his face, his arm is hurt, he needs stitches. Something really bad happened in that house. I tried to help him clean; he looked so lost, so alone. They have no food!" I was still struggling to catch my breath as the sobs racked my throat.

My mother put her arms around me, trying to console me and calm me down. "Lucy, Mrs. Nimchak has had her share of troubles, we know. Those boys will need all the good friends they can find to get them through this horrible time. You are a special friend to those boys. You did the right thing today, honey. I am very proud of you."

My mother stroked my hair as I sobbed.

"Please honey, pray with me," Mom said. "Hold my hands and close your eyes. Blessed Lord, please look over our friends and neighbors. Bring Jack and Charles strength and courage during this extremely difficult time. God bless them always and keep them safe. Amen."

My sobs subsided. "Amen," I said. My mother stood and kissed me on the forehead.

"Why don't you go upstairs and lay down. You've had a hard day, honey."

I walked upstairs and went to bed that night with my head aching. My mind so busy, thinking of Jack and how he was feeling at that moment. What was he doing? Was he scared?

The next day, I woke and quickly dressed. I had only one motive and that was to bring food to Jack and Charles. I ran out of the house with eggs and bread and more cookies my mother had baked the day before. I rushed down the street to the Nimchak house and banged on the door. No answer, but it was partially ajar and my banging had pushed it open. I walked into the house.

"Jack?" I said quietly so not to startle anyone. No answer. "JACK! CHARLES! Are you here?" Nothing. No one. I walked around the house. There was no one home. Everything felt empty. No sign of life. I left Jack a note.

Jack, I put some groceries in the fridge for you and Charles.

I know about your mother…I am so sorry, Jack. Please come see me as soon as you can. My heart is broken for you.

Love, Lucy.

I left the house that morning hopeful that I may see my friends. But Jack and Charles never came back home. They never returned to their house or the neighborhood again.

CHAPTER 6

Jack

I stood watching Lucy walk up the street toward her house. She turned twice to look back at me. I wished she could stay here. I felt safe with her. She doesn't know how sweet she is. How innocent. As I watched her to make sure she made it safely, I could see the car coming down the street. It was a police car. My stomach turned. Oh god, what do I do? Maybe it will pass. Maybe it's not meant for me. I waited, holding my breath. The car pulled straight into my driveway. I looked past it at Lucy. She stopped walking and was staring back at me. Then she turned and ran. She's scared. I could feel it and see it in her face. It's okay, Lucy, I thought to myself. I also wanted to turn and run in the other direction, but I couldn't. I was frozen with fear. I stood there, waiting.

"CHARLES!" I screamed. My brother exited the back of the police car. I opened the front door and ran down the steps to meet with him. "Charles! Where have you been?!" Charles looked up at me. His face was broken. He didn't smile. He said nothing.

"Hi Jack, my name is Officer Belden. You can call me Joseph." The officer approached me and shook my hand.

"Hello, Officer," I said, not taking my eyes off my brother.

"I want you boys to come into the house for a minute. I need to talk to you, Jack."

I hesitated. "Okay." I threw a darted glance at my brother. "Charles, what's wrong? Why are you acting like this? Why aren't you talking to me?"

"Come on, Jack," Charles said. "Let's go inside."

The three of us entered the living room of our small house. I was so thankful to Lucy for helping me clean earlier. Thank god! I sat on the couch. Charles sat next to me and held my hand. This was strange, I thought.

"Jack, has anyone taken a look at that nasty bruise on your face?" Officer Belden asked.

"Yes, my brother here brought me to Dr. Long a couple days back. I fell off my bike and I needed a few stitches," I lied.

"I see." The officer paused. "Well, I picked Charles up and he says he's been looking for your mother."

I looked at Charles. I looked for any sign from him; any signal that would alert me to what the hell was going on here.

"Jack, we have some bad news to tell you about your mother. She's dead, Jack. She has passed away," Officer Belden stated casually.

I heard the words. I saw the officer speaking, his hand reaching out to touch my shoulder, giving me his condolences. "I...I don't understand," I said. "Charles? What is he saying?"

Charles looked up at me, his eyes full of sorrow. He too appeared to be in shock. "Jack, she's gone. She's never coming back. She's left us forever," he stated, his voice angry. My mind was spinning. My stomach was nauseous. I stood to run to the bathroom.

I slammed the bathroom door and emptied my stomach, my body shivering and convulsing. Tears stinging my eyes as I tried to process what I had heard. I stood and looked at myself in the mirror. This couldn't be happening.

I slowly returned to the living room. Charles and Officer Belden were speaking quietly, my brother raising his voice occasionally. They both stopped to look at me.

"Are you okay, son?" Officer Belden asked.

I didn't answer him. "How did she die? Where did you find her? What's going to happen now?"

"Your brother and I were just discussing what we should do. Do either of you have any contact with your father?" the officer asked.

"No," we both said in unison.

"We could stay here," I suggested.

"We can get jobs," Charles added.

"I understand that the two of you would like to remain here, in your home. That's something that's not possible, boys. You can't live here by yourselves; you're too young."

"That's bullshit!" Charles said. He paced the room back and forth, kicking over one of the ottomans in frustration.

I looked at Officer Belden, an elderly gentleman. I could see he felt for us, but he probably had a family of his own that he would like to return to.

"Where will we go?" I asked. Silence. "What about my mother's father, Grandpa Lou?"

"Oh! You have a grandfather?" Officer Belden asked.

"Shut up, Jack!" Charles yelled.

"Yes, we have a grandfather. He lives out west. He runs a farm," I said. "What about him, does he know Mom has died?"

"No, I don't believe so, Jack," Officer Belden replied.

"What happened to her?" I asked again.

"She was murdered, Jack!" Charles screamed. "By the same son of a bitch who blackened your eye!"

I slumped down on the couch, defeated. This was entirely my fault. Why did I push him? Why didn't I just keep my mouth shut?

"Okay, okay boys. Let's take it easy tonight. This is a lot to digest. I have a woman waiting for you down at the station. She's going to help you get settled for the evening. We'll talk again tomorrow and try to contact your grandfather. We'll see what we can do for you boys. Why don't you round up a couple of your belongings and you can come with me?"

I stood and followed Charles into our bedroom. Charles looked at me. He had a hard look on his face.

"I'm not going to stay with Grandpa Lou, Jack. He's never met us. He's a stranger," Charles argued with me, worry evident in his wrinkled eyebrows.

"What are you going to do, Charles? We don't have a lot of choices here."

47

"I know, but I'll think of something. Grab your things and let's go."

I did what I was told. I was tired, exhausted from the entire day. I couldn't think straight. I wish I could talk to Lucy. Maybe talk to her mother. They would offer good advice.

Charles and I sat in the back of the police car. We made our way down to the police station. No one spoke in the vehicle. Charles stared outside the window, his face angry. Mrs. Nelson was waiting for us when we got there.

"Hello, Jack. Hello, Charles. My name is Mrs. Nelson. I'm very sorry to hear about your mother," she said.

"Hello," I said. Charles said nothing.

"I need to separate you boys tonight. I'm very sorry to do this, but it's the only housing I could find on such short notice. Tomorrow we will meet again to see where you will be temporarily staying," she explained. Charles looked at me, disgusted. He snickered and shook his head.

"Where are you taking my brother?" he asked.

Mrs. Nelson looked at Charles, her eyes soft. It was clear she was a nice lady, but the look on Charles' face seemed to say that he couldn't care less. "Jack will be staying with a young couple; they have a three-year-old son. It's a nice family; you needn't worry. You'll be staying with an elderly couple.

They've raised a family and have grown children. They like to help children like you, who are in need. Both families are waiting for you downstairs. Is there anything else I can do for you boys tonight? Anything you need?"

"Yeah. We'd like to go home," Charles stated.

"I'm sorry Charles, that's not going to happen."

"Jack?" Mrs. Nelson looked at me.

"No, ma'am. Thank you for your time and your concern. Your arrangement seems fine for tonight," I said respectfully. Mrs. Nelson led us out of the office and walked us downstairs.

"I suggest you two say your goodbyes for now."

I looked at Charles. My eyes started to burn again. My throat was in a knot. I grabbed my brother. I hugged him hard. Charles looked into my face.

"It's going to be alright, Jack. I promise you."

"I love you, Charles."

"I love you too, Jack."

That was the last time I saw my brother.

The next morning, Mrs. Nelson arrived at my foster family's home. We sat in the living room to talk. She seemed very nervous.

"Jack, it appears that Charles has run away," she stated.

"What!? When?"

"We're pretty sure he left last night. There was no note, nothing."

I couldn't believe it. My brother left without me. "What does this mean?"

"Well, the police are out looking for him now. We hope we can catch up with him. We're going to do our best to find Charles. Do you have any ideas where he might have gone?"

I thought about my brother. How angry he looked last night. I assumed he went back to our house, stayed one last night, and then jumped on his dirt bike and drove off somewhere.

"He wouldn't do well in foster care," I told Mrs. Nelson. Charles was wild, a free spirit; he needed to work on bikes and race and do whatever he pleased. We hadn't answered to my mother in years. How was Charles supposed to handle having new parents to answer to? He was too old for that now. "I truly don't know where he would go, Mrs. Nelson. We have no other family."

"Well, Jack, I do have some promising news for you." She smiled, clearly pleased with herself for finding a solution. "Your grandfather has been notified and he has agreed to come and take you back to his home. He will be your custodian."

"Okay," I said nervously. I had no idea what to expect from Grandpa Lou. My mother only talked about him on rare occasions when she was sober. She talked about the farm she grew up on, and how her father would take her fishing. After my mother's parents divorced, her mother wouldn't allow her to see her father. Her mother was an alcoholic and my mother, also an alcoholic.

"Well, I appreciate that he is willing to take me in," I said slowly, maturely. "I would rather stay here in town, to find my brother."

"Your grandfather would like both of you boys with him. As soon as we find Charles, he will be going too," Mrs. Nelson added. "We will do our best, Jack."

This week couldn't get any worse. "What about my mother?" I asked.

"Your grandfather will be handling the funeral arrangements. He will be here later this afternoon. You can help him with that. I'll need you to come with me now, and we'll wait for him at the station."

I said thank you to my foster family and Mrs. Nelson and I left in her vehicle. As we drove through town, I had an overwhelming feeling that I would never see this place again. Not for a long time. I looked for Charles down the alleyways, at the gas station, hoping to catch a glimpse of him. I knew they would never find him. He was gone. I was on my own now.

My grandfather was waiting for us when we arrived at the station. He must have driven all night to get to Connecticut. He was a big man, strong. Not what I had envisioned.

"Hey Jack," Grandpa Lou said as he reached for my hand and shook it.

"Hi, Grandpa," I said carefully.

"God, you look like my brother. Your uncle Bobby."

I've never heard of Uncle Bobby but my grandfather had a strong grip.

"Mrs. Nelson, is there some paperwork I need to fill out, any forms?"

"There are no forms for you to take Jack home, Mr. Nimchak. You are the next of kin and his grandfather. He can leave with you," she answered.

My grandfather sat down next to me and placed his hand on my shoulder. "Jack, I would like to bring your mother back home. I would like to bury her on the farm, in a quiet place under the oak tree where she used to play as a little girl. I think she would really like that. She loved our farm," he said. Grandpa looked down at the ground, remembering my mother, his eyes sad and full of regret. "I missed a lot of time with your mother, with you boys. I know it's been difficult," he said.

I'm not sure what I'm supposed to do. "It's okay, Grandpa," I said.

"Please, Jack...call me Pop."

CHAPTER 7

Charles

Charles sat up in his unfamiliar bed and stared through the window, where he could see the moon shining and the trees out in the distance. He stood and looked down into the street of the unfamiliar neighborhood. His stomach lurched and twisted with every breath he took. He couldn't visualize living here. He couldn't gather his thoughts around his mother's death, or Jack. How could he take care of his brother? All he wanted was to feel free, to do something familiar and comfortable. He wanted his dirt bike. He wanted to jump on it and ride away into the sunset, never to be seen again.

He dressed and crept out into the hallway. His foster caregivers were elderly, probably deep sleepers. He made his way down the carpeted stairwell, grateful to be walking on the soft flooring as opposed to the hardwood he was accustomed to in his home. He slipped through the kitchen and outside of the back door.

Charles made his way downtown and hitched a ride to his neighborhood. He ran into the house and collapsed in the center floor of his living room. The overwhelming emotion of desperation and sadness overcame him and he wept, his hands covering his face, the guttural noises of pain and heartache escaping his chest as he cried.

Hours passed as he mourned his mother, his home, his brother. Soothed, exhausted, he stood from the living room floor and walked into the kitchen. He paused and looked around at the cabinets, the table and the sink that had never looked so tidy. He walked through the dining room and paused, looking at the pictures that hung on the wall, some neatly, some crooked. He grabbed one picture of his brother and him and shoved it into his backpack. He wandered around the house, trying to remember everything, trying to capture every last moment.

Charles stood at the front door with his hand on the doorknob and turned to look one final time. He closed his eyes tight, wiping away the last tears that escaped them.

"Sorry Jack," he said. "I'm so sorry."

CHAPTER 8

Jack

I spent much of my time staring out of the window on our way out west. I had never been out of our town before, let alone out of our state. The city and the landscape changes were all new to me. My grandfather was quiet. He drove and listened to the AM station on the radio.

"How much longer, Pop?" I would ask shyly.

"It's a long drive, Jack. We'll get there, when we get there," Pop would reply. Great answer, I thought to myself.

I tried not to think about what happened to my mother. I tried to think of some happy moments, some good times with her. She wasn't always a bad person. She wasn't always so screwed up. There was that one time she took us to the ski mountain. No one in our family knew how to ski, certainly not my mother. I think her boyfriend at the time got it into her head.

"It's good for the boys, good for their bodies and minds," he would preach. I liked that guy. What was his name? Can't remember. But, she took us. She was sober that day. She bought our ski lift tickets and rented the equipment. My brother and I were young. I remember her standing at the bottom of the hill while Charles and I came barreling down out of control.

She would run and scream, "Oh god! Oh my god!" She would try to grab us before we hit anyone, fell, or got hurt. My brother and I would laugh. We thought it was great. How much fun we had. My mother was exhausted. She ran herself silly, trying to catch us. She never did take us again after that. But, I remember it. It was a good day.

"Pop? What happened to Mom, how did she die?" I blurted. I wasn't sure if I could handle the answer, but I asked it anyway.

Pop looked at me, seemingly trying to decide whether he should tell me. He let out a big sigh.

"She loved you boys. She really did. I hope you realize that she did her best. She just couldn't conquer her demons. Do you understand that, Jack? Do you understand she had a sickness?"

"She was sick?" I frowned. "What kind of sickness? Like cancer?"

"No, Jack." He paused and looked at me pointedly. "Alcoholism."

It would be another ten years before I really understood what alcoholism was. "I know she drank, Pop. She drank every day. Charles and I would sometimes steal money from our neighbors, just so they wouldn't shut off the electricity."

Pop kept his eyes on the road. "Did your mother work?"

"She did when we were younger, but not since my tenth birthday. She lost her job or was fired. I remember this because she had promised a big huge celebration for my birthday. Made a big deal about me turning ten. It never happened. She never left her room that day. She occasionally yelled for Charles to go buy her some more cigarettes." I flinched as I recalled the painful memory.

My grandfather shook his head. "Well, I'm sorry to hear that." I looked at my Pop's face. He looked defeated, regretful. "They found your mother in an abandoned apartment building. They're not quite sure how she died. It appeared that she might have overdosed on some sort of drugs or alcohol. They'll do an autopsy."

I closed my eyes. I swallowed hard trying to fight back my tears. I started to cry.

My grandfather turned to look at me. "This isn't your fault. You were a good boy, helping your mother all these years. She was sick. She couldn't help herself."

I nodded my head, agreeing with my grandfather. I needed to cry. It was all I could do. It was my fault, but it wasn't. I understood this. Charles was gone. My home was gone. My mother was gone. What else could I do? I felt so empty. I had no one, nothing left. So, I cried. I cried for a long time.

CHAPTER 9

Mama

Worry. Mama constantly worried. Any more worrying and she would eventually collapse on the ground. Her children standing above her, shaking their heads. "Who's going to do our laundry now?" they would ask.

Mama stared into the air, willing herself to get up and start dinner. If she didn't move now, she would never get up. She hated dinner. How she hated dinner. The children sat at the table, complaining about the meal. Talking loudly, arguing with one another. She couldn't wait for it to be over, the table cleared, bedtime near. She looked forward to the time when all her children were cleaned and tucked into their beds. She needed peace, when she could finally climb under her blankets and lay back on her pillows. It was her favorite time of the day, when she could stop worrying.

Mama thought about Lucy. What was she going to do about her? She was so sweet and sensitive. She was too mature for her age; she knew too much. Mama wanted to keep her young. She couldn't tell her about Jack. Lucy would worry about him forever if she let her. It was best to let her try to forget. Mama told her he was fine. Not to worry. Lucy didn't need to know Jack was with his grandfather now, a great place for him. He was safe and cared for. She didn't need to worry. Charles was gone. Nothing she could do for him now.

Mama had to make dinner. Daddy would be home soon. She wondered how his day went. He worked so hard. She would have to get up now. She needed to make him a nice dinner. He would enjoy it. He would be the only one.

CHAPTER 10

Jack

A box came today, shipped from Connecticut. The box said "Jack Nimchak" C/O Lou Nimchak THE ESTATE OF DONNA NIMCHAK. The box apparently held everything of value that belonged to my mother. It was a small box. Pop placed it on my bed. He told me to open it when I was ready. I opened it. There were pictures of my brother, my mother and I. There was one nice one of her. I taped it to my mirror. There were a few books and a small notebook my mother had. She wrote numbers and bills and dollar amounts in it. She must have tried to keep track of the household bills. I quickly went through the box and then pulled out a note. I couldn't believe what it was. It was from Lucy.

Jack, I put some groceries in the fridge for you and Charles.

I know about your mother…I am so sorry, Jack. Please come see me as soon as you can. My heart is broken for you.

Love, Lucy.

I held the note to my chest. I wish I could reach out to her but my Pop thought I should try to move on. I would never forget what she did for me that day. How she took care of me. The memories came rushing back, the way she looked at me while we cleaned our broken down, battered home. The look on Lucy's face haunted me, the way she looked as she watched the cop car drive by her. I read Lucy's note. I folded it neatly and placed it in the drawer next to my bed.

"Jack!" my grandfather yelled.

"Yeah, Pop?"

"Let's go, son. There's work to do!"

"Be right there!" I closed the box and pushed it under my bed. One box. One small box.

I walked outside to meet up with my grandfather. He was talking with the farm hands, telling them what he wanted accomplished for the day. Three men worked for my grandfather. Along with Susie Mae, our housekeeper. She cooked and cleaned and tended to the smaller animals, the chickens, rabbits, and goats. When I first arrived at the farm, my grandfather placed me under her care. She brought me with her while she did her chores and let me feed the chickens and gather the eggs.

My grandfather's farm was beautiful. The white farmhouse with black shutters, lined with picket fences and glorious flower gardens all around, was something I had never seen before. The wide-open spaces, a far cry from our tiny home and yard back in Connecticut. And the barns! Meticulously kept barns full of animals and feed, tractors and equipment, a dream come true. My only wish would be for Charles to see it here, see what he has missed.

"You keep your eye on the rooster, you hear me boy?" Susie would say to me.

"Yeah, yeah, yeah," I said, rolling my eyes. Boy, did I have a lot to learn. I turned my back just one time, and that rooster flew right at me, pecking at me, flapping its wings.

Susie Mae came running into the chicken coop with her broom. "Damn bird! I told you to watch him, Jack."

"I'm sorry. I had no idea that bird could fly so high!"

"Well, be more careful next time. He'll take your eye out."

"Yes, ma'am," I replied, embarrassed.

I learned quickly on the farm. My grandfather's friends would come and say, "You've got yourself quite a boy, Lou, a strong hand. We need that kind of young energy around here." My grandfather would sit back and smile. He was proud to have a grandson. I tried hard not to disappoint him. Pop took a lot of care to show me all the equipment. Teach me everything he could about farming. I often thought that Charles would have loved it here. There was so much machinery. So much he could have done and contributed to. Charles was great at that sort of thing.

I walked outside to meet up with my grandfather.

"Come on, Jack. I want you to come with me today. I think you've learned all you can about the chicken coop."

"Sure! I'm ready." I jumped down from the porch. Pop threw me the keys to his truck.

"Hop in, son," he said with a smirk. I stopped and stared at him. Was he crazy? He wanted me to drive?

"Are you sure, Pop?" I asked, hesitating.

"Yup. Hop in, boy. I'll need someone to drive me around soon enough. I can't drive forever."

A smile spread across my face. I jumped into the old truck and started the engine. My grandfather got into the passenger side.

"Now, this here old truck is a little rough and fragile. You need to take her slowly and treat her nicely." Pop rubbed his hand along the dashboard. "Shift her in gear and press on the gas, nice and easy."

I did what my grandfather told me. I had never driven a car before. There was that one time when Charles and I stole the neighbor's beat-up Chevy and took it for a joy ride. Charles drove; I never did get a chance. We were too scared and nervous. We took the Chevy around the block and then parked it sideways in my neighbor's driveway. He came to complain to my mother, but that was pointless. My mother just told him, "Go to hell! Not my boys!"

"Head up the road," Pop instructed. "I want to show you the land and the boundaries of the farm."

"Can we get in trouble for this?" I asked nervously.

My grandfather gave me a look. "Just drive, Jack. You don't need to worry about those things. I'm the adult here," he said firmly.

"Okay." I drove up the road past the cornfields, which seemed to go on for miles. I drove past McFlynn's Pump & Pay, the tiny gas station conveniently situated in the middle of nowhere. I drove past Charlie's Mechanic Shop with old retired farm equipment littering the parking lot waiting to be serviced or parts reused in another's restoration. I drove past Mama Bev's Farm Stand, the local harvest of corn and vegetables evident in her displays. Across the street was the entrance to The White Flower Farm, the huge images of steel farm silos filling the skyline.

"Take a right here, Jack, on this dirt road. Do you see it?"

"Yup, got it." I turned onto the dirt road and followed it along the backside of the cornfields. The dirt road was rugged and hilly.

"Take your time, just ease her over the rough spots. All this land, son, is our farm," Pop explained. "Pretty soon we will come to the top of the hill, where you can see it in its entirety."

I was interested in seeing the farm, but I was trying hard to concentrate on driving the truck. I never drove a truck before and I certainly didn't want to disappoint Pop now, now that he trusted me. It wasn't until I reached the top of the hill that I realized the magnitude and vastness of my grandfather's land.

"Pull over here, Jack."

I parked the truck and my grandfather and I exited the vehicle.

It was spectacular. "Over there is the house. You can see Susie Mae! See her?" My grandfather laughed. "Over there to the east are the cow pastures, and to the right of that are the apple orchards. There's Albert and Johnson, fixing the fence to the south. One of our cows went loose last night. Found her up at the Benson Farm, five miles down the road. Damn cow."

My grandfather spoke quickly and excitedly. He was a proud man; he had every reason to be. I stood and listened, trying to keep up. Why did my mother ever leave this place?

"Wow, Pop, look at the pond. You can see everything from here. All the barns, all the livestock." I was truly impressed. Pop looked down at me, smiled, and placed his hand on my shoulder. For the first time I felt safe, I felt like I belonged somewhere. Like I mattered and could be important. I looked at my grandfather. "Thank you...thank you for bringing me here, for taking care of me."

"You're my son now, Jack. I love you, boy."

I smiled.

"Come on now, let's not get all mushy. There's more for you to see and we've got work to do today. Get back in that truck." Pop wrapped his arm around me.

"Let's go," I said with a renewed sense of life in my heart.

CHAPTER 11

Lucy

Years passed and the memories from that day faded. I harassed my mother for a long time about Jack and Charles, but she told me she never could find out what happened to them. I thought about Jack often. I wished he were here, experiencing the same boring classes in high school that I was, attending prom and trying to get a driver's license. We were graduating high school soon; senior year was eventful and my social life was becoming very important to me. I was constantly on the phone talking to my girlfriends. My mother was constantly irritated with me. But I didn't care. There were important things going on. Things she couldn't understand.

"Lucy!" Mom screamed. "Get off that damn phone!"

Ugh! I sighed. We had one phone in the entire house and it was in the kitchen. I had found a convenient quiet place underneath our dining room table to talk with my friends, but

69

my mother didn't appreciate the cord running from the kitchen to the dining room.

"A couple minutes, Mom!" I yelled from beneath the table. I turned back to the phone. "So, Amelia? What happened after Mr. Bulky found out your were missing from gym period?"

"Lucy, you know I hate gym. Hate it! Hate it! Hate it! So when Mrs. Tiny wanted a volunteer to hang the posters for prom, I obviously raised my hand!"

Amelia was my best, best, best friend in the whole world. She was beautiful and sassy. The boys were crazy about her. She had beautiful teeth, no braces, beautiful skin, no acne, beautiful hair and eyes. She was petite and sweet and wildly popular. She was very aggressive and confident, but that's why I loved her. Mrs. Tiny was not really Mrs. Tiny. That's just a name Amelia came up with to describe what she obviously wasn't.

"So, I didn't tell Mrs. Tiny I had skipped gym class to help her. I told her Mr. Bulky was okay with the idea." Mr. Bulky wasn't very bulky either.

"Well, what happened when you didn't show up for class?" I was afraid that Amelia would jeopardize her chance to go to the dance.

"I was called down to the principal's office and Mr. Bulky, Mrs. Tiny, and Principal Cray-Cray were all sitting there," she answered.

"Oh my god! What happened?" I asked. The suspense was killing me.

My mother's shrill voice interrupted us. "*Lucy!* Get off the phone! Right now!"

I poked my head out from underneath the tablecloth. "Please, *Mom!* It's very important." I turned back to the phone again, this time anxious. "Amelia, you need to talk quickly! My mother is having a conniption!"

"Okay, okay! So, long story short. I'm on probation and I'm not allowed any more chances. No stories about where I am and where I'm going or I'll be in school suspension. No dance!"

"Okay, phew. You need to promise me you'll stay out of trouble, Amelia," I scolded.

"I'll try my best." She giggled.

"I got to go," I said. "See you in class tomorrow!"

"Bye, Lucy! Good luck!"

When I appeared from underneath the dining table, Thomas was standing there, waiting for me. Everybody was home that day. The house was louder and crazier than ever. Mikey was off in the distance somewhere breaking something and Mom was in a yelling mood.

"Kaylan, get in here and clean your mess off this floor! I'm not everyone's damn maid!" my mother yelled. Julia was cooking dinner for Mom, as she often did. Julia did everything Mom couldn't, including helping with our homework, laundry, and dinner. As hard and difficult as Julia could be, you had to feel sorry for her. She had a lot of extra chores that the rest of us didn't, and she sure wasn't happy about it.

"Lucy?" Julia asked. "Can you set the table?"

"Yeah sure," I said as I tried to step into the kitchen. Of course, I forgot about Tommy. Tommy was standing waiting for me, blocking my entrance. I tried to step around him, but he stepped in front of me again. Back and forth we did this.

Tommy, over the years, has grown into a large young man, 6'2" and counting. Finally, my patience got to me.

"Thomas, what the hell?" I said. "Get out of my way, I need to set the table."

"No Lucy! I need to talk to you about Amelia."

"She's not interested in you, Tommy!" I muttered, irritated.

"You're way too old for her, Tommy," Julia added. "Really, I'm sure there are plenty of girls your age who want to date you. There's no need to stalk Lucy's one and only friend."

"Yeah," I said. "Now, *move!*"

Tommy grabbed my wrist and bent down to talk to me in my face. "Did you ask her? What did she say?"

"She said you're a disgusting pig! She would rather sit all year in detention than go out on a date with you!"

Tommy had a bit of a short fuse, and this did not sit well with him. Tommy was in fact very sought after by many, many girls. He was a big boy, handsome to look at and a fantastic baseball player. He was home visiting from Boston College where he played ball and studied politics. I didn't tell Amelia my dumb brother was in love with her; I would rather die. Amelia would have been thrilled to death, but no way!

"Move, Tommy. I need to help Julia."

Rather than move, Tommy picked me up and held me high over his head like a bag of potatoes. He then proceeded to drop me flat on my back on the hard wooden floor. My mind went blank and numb as the air in my lungs escaped my chest. I tried to get up, but could not catch my breath. I couldn't cry or speak or breathe.

I slowly began to move and noticed the drips and spots of blood, all over my shirt, all over the floor. My eyes went wide as I gasped for the air that was slowly returning to my lungs. I glanced down and around my body. I needed to find where the blood was coming from.

Then, there it was. Tommy, holding his head while the blood trickled out of his forehead, my sister Julia, holding the receiver of the phone in her hand, the obvious choice of weapon. Julia stood much shorter than my brother and showed no fear or hesitation. She held the phone receiver in her hand tightly, not willing to let go of the object of defense, and then moved up on her tippy toes and put her finger in Tommy's face. She spoke in a very angry and determined voice.

"*Don't* touch her again!"

Tommy looked down at my sister, realizing what he had done and decided it was not in his best interest to push Julia. He grabbed a towel and held it to his head.

"You effin' bitch, Julia. I didn't mean to hurt her," he growled.

"You better drag ass, Tommy, before Dad comes in here," Julia warned. Tommy glared at Julia and me. With that threat, he left.

Julia helped me to my feet. "Are you okay?" she asked.

"Oh my god. What the hell was that?"

"He's a jerk, Lucy. Keep your distance from him."

"Thank you." I stood, dazed. "I don't even know why he did that. He's obsessed with Amelia."

"He did that because he's an asshole." Julia turned and walked back to the stove to finish dinner as if nothing had happened. I could never quite figure her out. She hated me, she helped me, she loved me, and I really annoyed her. All I know is that she had my back that day, and I was grateful.

My brother Thomas changed after that incident. I assumed he had gotten a new girlfriend because his attitude toward me was pleasant, his efforts kind and generous. I had never seen him so happy, in fact. Things were going well for him. School was good; he was engrossed in his baseball career, his classmates and friends.

I, on the other hand, had bigger things to concern myself with. Amelia and I were having the best of times. She was able to behave herself long enough to attend senior prom without getting suspended. We shopped for days looking for the right dresses. We wondered which boys would ask us to dance. I had to laugh at Amelia because *all* of the boys would ask her to dance. She looked great in *all* of the dresses she tried on. I, on the other hand, felt skinny and boyish.

Amelia would say to me, "Lucy, you're perfect! You're perfect just the way you are."

I didn't feel perfect. My mother called me Skinny Minnie Me. I guess I reminded her of herself at my age. I hoped that I could grow up to look like my mother—she was beautiful. But for now, I would like to fill out a prom dress, without stuffing my bra. I would like to have a little bit of shape to myself.

Amelia finally narrowed her dress options down to two dresses. One was pink. One was blue. She looked stunning in both.

"Amelia, the blue one shows off your blue sparkly eyeballs," I said, looking up at her pretty face.

She giggled. "Eyeballs, Lucy?"

"Yes, eyeballs. They *sparkle*!"

"Okay, Lucy. I suppose I should get the blue dress." Amelia tossed the dress aside and picked out another dress, one I would never dare try on. "Lucy! Please, please, please? Try this one? For me, Lucy?"

"Oh stop it, Amelia. You're ridiculous."

"*Please?*" she begged. I started to laugh. I could never say no to Amelia. She was just ridiculous and fun.

"Okay! Amelia, okay!"

"Hurray!" Amelia shuffled me into the dressing room, plopped the dress down, and said, "Hurry up now."

"Get out," I said as I shoved her slightly, laughing.

How did I let her con me into these things? I quickly undressed in order to get this embarrassment over with. I looked at myself in the mirror and I sighed, a heavy sigh. Boyish, I thought. *At least my hair looks decent.* I pulled the dress on over my hips and over my chest. The dress was full of pleats and lace. Slightly fitted at my waist and then flared over my hips to just above my knees. The bodice was tight and fitted and I was greatly appreciative for the extra padding in the chest. *I think I like it,* I thought. *Oh, what do I know?*

"Amelia?" I started to exit the dressing room, my eyes glued to the floor. "What do you think?"

Amelia sprung up from her seat. Her excitement was overflowing. "I love it, Lucy! You look fabulous. Don't you think so? It's really, really beautiful on you!"

"Are you sure, Amelia? It's not too much?"

"Not at all. You have to buy it. Your mother will love it."

My mother. She doesn't really want me to buy a new dress. I should be wearing one of my sister's older dresses, but I've been working and I can help to pay for it.

"It's $200, Amelia. My mother is going to worry about that."

"Lucy, you work so hard. All you do is babysit and help out your family. You deserve your own dress for the dance." She grinned.

"I guess so." I started to smile. *I really like my dress,* I thought. I opened my purse to count how much money I had. "I have exactly $210."

"That's great!"

"Amelia, promise me you won't tell my mother. I'm going to tell her it cost $75."

"Yeah sure. *No problemo.*"

"Great! I'm going to buy it then. Are you ready to go?"

"Yeah. What do you say we stop by the basketball courts on our way home? See if there's any action going on."

"We'll have to ask Tommy, and I have to be home for dinner. I need to help my mother with supper."

We made our purchases. I felt excited and confident about my dress. We waited outside the dress shop for Tommy to pick us up. The only time he offered to drive me anywhere was if Amelia was going as well. He still had a huge crush on Amelia, even though I was certain he was involved with someone else. My brother's constant trips home from Boston appeased my mother's need to see him on occasion and was helpful because he was able to drive me around once in awhile. My family was proud of him.

"Here comes Tommy, Amelia. Just ignore him, he's so dopey around you."

"Oh stop it, Lucy. Your brother is nothing but sweet to me. Always has been. I don't know why you give him such a hard time."

"That's just disgusting, Amelia." We laughed and giggled as we climbed in to the back seat of the car. I nearly choked and died when I realized who was sitting in the front seat next to Tommy.

"Charles!" I exclaimed. "What! What are you doing here?"

Charles glanced back at me, not nearly as shocked to see me as I was to see him.

"I ran into Charles today, down at the loading plant where he's been working," Tommy said. "Wasn't I surprised to see you, Charles?"

As Charles and Tommy talked back and forth, I stared at Charles, hardly believing that he was here.

"What happened, Charles? What happened to you and Jack? Where's Jack?" I asked, the tone of my desperation for so many years creeping into my voice.

"Geez, Lucy. What's with all the questions? Give the man a little space. I just picked him up. We're going to catch up after we drop you little turkeys off," Tommy said.

Charles glanced down at the floor of the car. "Yeah, can't wait to catch up with you, Tommy. It's been a long time."

I grabbed hold of the back of the headrest and nearly flung myself into the front seat with the two boys. "Charles, I need to know. Is Jack okay? I've thought of you and Jack so often. I would really like to know what happened. Where did you go? Are you all okay?"

"Lucy, take it easy," Amelia said. She placed her hands on my hips and forced me to sit down. I looked back at her. *She doesn't understand.*

Tommy turned the corner and headed down the street toward our house. He asked Charles, "Would you like to take a ride past your old house, buddy?"

Charles looked up, his face very still, his body language showing no emotion. "No Tommy, I wouldn't."

Tommy shrugged. "Okay. You two twerps can get out of the car now." Tommy stopped and parked in front of my house to let us off. I opened the door and stopped at Charles' door. He rolled down the window and looked at me.

"Please Charles, is Jack okay?" I asked softly. Charles paused for a minute and then looked up at me, shaking his head.

"Lucy, I really don't know. We were separated years ago. I haven't seen my brother since my mother died. I'm sorry, Lucy."

Charles rolled the window up and my brother Tommy slowly pulled the car away. Amelia and I stood there watching as the car moved down the street.

"What was that all about?" Amelia asked.

"It's a long story, Amelia. I don't really want to talk about it."

"Okie dokie, Lulu beans," she said. Amelia always tried to make me laugh. "Come on. Let's go inside and try on our dresses for everyone." Amelia grabbed my arm as she tried to regain my attention.

I stood there watching the car as it turned the corner, down the road.

I sighed deeply. "Okay, Amelia, let's have our fashion show." I was happy for the distraction, but seeing Charles again brought back so many thoughts about that day with Jack and the tragedy of his mother. How did the boys get separated? Did my mother know? She always assured me that they were fine. What did she know? Nothing, maybe. Maybe she tried to find out, but couldn't. *I don't know,* I thought. It's all so confusing and frustrating. It was nice to see Charles. When Tommy gets home, I'll find out more information. There's got to be more.

CHAPTER 12

Lucy

Thomas came home that evening after catching up with Charles. He was tired and annoyed with Kathryn. I wasn't sure why, but he definitely wasn't interested in my fifty questions. I told my mother we saw Charles. She didn't appear to be surprised.

"Lucy, honey, I've told you a hundred times already, Jack and Charles are fine," she said without concern.

"Well, I would like to talk to Jack myself."

"That's nonsense. I'm too busy here with you kids to be chasing down other kids 'just because,'" she said as she busied herself. It didn't seem likely that my mother knew where Jack was other than that she had been reassured that he was in a safe place. That's all my mother would ever be concerned about—whether you were safe, fed, clean, and healthy. That you were happy was not what she worried about. "Please Lucy, I'm busy. Can we just put this to rest?"

"Fine!" I spat. I was not okay with it but it was evident that no one else in my family seemed to care.

Kathryn was home, which was a rare thing nowadays. I walked up the stairs toward our bedroom and knocked on her door. She was sitting on her bed, listening to her headphones and writing in her journal. Kathryn was somewhat of a hippy, a free spirit. She was easygoing. She didn't mind me moping around her room, touching her things.

"Hey Lulu! What's up, buttercup?" she said happily. I smiled. "Sit with me!" Kathryn said as she moved over on her bed. "Tell me what you think of this new album I bought. You can sit here and listen." I sat next to Kathryn while she put her headphones on my head. It felt funny, those bulky headphones, but it made her happy. I sat and listened while she watched me, waiting for my expression to change. I nodded and gave her double thumbs up.

"Nice! Right, Lucy? Do you like it?"

"Yes Kathryn. What is it?" I asked.

"It's the Grateful Dead."

The Grateful Dead. My sister loved music and concerts. My parents worried for Kathryn because she didn't seem to have a goal or plan for her life. She graduated high school a few years back and had no intentions of moving on or out or going to college. My sister Julia had left the year before and Tommy was a sophomore at Boston College. Kathryn was content coming and going and "enjoying *life*, Mom!" as she would say. Kathryn was a bit of a mystery in this family. She never brought her friends home and you didn't quite know what she was doing or who she was with. It exasperated my mother, but it was what it was. I appreciated the rare times I could spend with her, when she was willing to hang out and shoot the breeze.

"So, what's up? What's on your mind, Lucy? Any boys in your life?" she pried.

"*No!*" I said, disgusted. I gathered my thoughts. "Well actually, Amelia and I are going to the prom together. There will be lots of boys there. We like to flirt and giggle and be silly with some of them but nothing serious. You know what I mean, Kathryn? No one interests me; I can't seem to get into dating." I stood and moved toward her dresser, sizing up one of Kathryn's shirts against my chest, staring at myself in her mirror, watching Kathryn's reflection at the same time.

"Yeah, that's the best way to be, Lucy. Boys are no good. You enjoy your girlfriends, have fun, hang out...nothing serious."

"What about you?" I asked as I turned to face her. "You're always so secretive."

"I know. A girl likes her privacy. It's not necessary to share every feeling or thought you have with every single person you know," she lectured. I nodded to indicate that I was paying attention to her. "Hey, do you want to go for a walk with me? We'll tell Mom we're going blueberry picking, but I don't want Jess or Kaylan to come, definitely not Mikey. Okay?" she asked.

"Yeah, sure!" I answered excitedly.

"Okay. Grab a jacket and meet me outside."

I was so excited my sister actually wanted to hang with me. It seemed so out of character considering she spent all of her time away from our family. Once we were out of Mom's sight, my sister opened up her coat and took out a pack of smokes. She took one, lit it and handed it to me then lit another one for herself. "Kathryn, I didn't know you smoked!" I said, surprised.

"I do sometimes. Not all the time, and that's not all I have but you need to promise me that this is between you and I. I will never trust you again if you can't keep this secret." My sister reached into her cigarette pack and took out a joint. I wasn't even sure what it was. "This is pot, Lucy," she said with a smile. You smoke it like you're sucking the air out of a balloon." I stared at my sister in shock as I watched the demonstration.

We walked past the pond to the waterfall. We sat on a boulder and she lit the joint and handed it to me. I tried my best to act as cool as I could. I tried to pretend I knew how to smoke it and tried my best not to cough.

"You're such an amateur," Kathryn laughed. "It takes a few tries before you get the hang of it."

"So, is this what you and your friends do? Smoke pot and cigarettes?" I asked.

"Yeah, and other things."

I passed the joint back to Kathryn and a strange sensation started to overcome me. My arms began to tingle and my chest burned as a blanket of relaxation began to fulfill me. A sense of joy and happiness began to encase me, and a consistent smile spread across my face.

"Kathryn, look at that silly squirrel chasing that other silly squirrel," I observed. Kathryn started to laugh.

"Yeah, they are very strange animals. All they do is chase each other."

I couldn't stop giggling. "Kathryn, we are going to get in so much trouble."

"Don't worry, Lucy. We'll hang here till we're ready to go home."

"Okay."

"So Lulu Belle, tell me, there must be someone you think about, some boy who interests you?" Kathryn asked, as she looked at me curiously. I was feeling good, not wanting to ruin my buzz.

Jack popped into my head. It's always Jack. "Do you remember Jack and Charles Nimchak?"

"Those cute boys that lived down the street?"

"Yes."

"Yeah, what about them?"

"I always think of Jack," I said softly.

"*Ohh*, I see. You have a crush on him." Kathryn gave my arm a little shove, a little too hard. I fell off the rock.

"Kathryn!" I yelled from the ground. I started laughing. She didn't mean it. Kathryn jumped off the rock and helped me to my feet.

"Lucy! Oh my god. You're like a soft, little feather, so light the wind could blow you over!" We were both laughing now. Kathryn gave me a hug. "I love you, Lucy. You're the best!"

"I love you too, Kathryn. Thanks for teaching me how to smoke pot!" I teased.

"Why don't we start to head back home and you can tell me all about Jack?"

I nodded. "We better stop off and bring Mom some blueberries. She'll wonder where we've been all this time. Plus, I'm soooo hungry and thirsty."

"Oh yeah! The blueberries! Good thinking, Luce." We walked back toward our house, arm in arm. Years later, I'd think back to this special moment with my sister. Even though she wasn't around much, she showed interest in my life. I didn't obtain enough information about her life other than how she spent her time doing drugs with her friends. I should have asked more questions. I wish I asked more questions.

CHAPTER 13

Kathryn

Kathryn thought about Lucy and the afternoon she spent at her parents' house. She walked into Demetry's kitchen and threw her bag up onto the counter. She sat down at the kitchen table, exhausted by her thoughts of Lucy and her family. She wished she could confide in someone. Her feelings were so torn and confused. She had no one to talk to besides Demetry, her best friend, a savior, and his home was her safe haven where she could continue living the secret life that she'd been hiding from her family for so long.

Demetry and Kat grew up together and had many things in common. Demetry had secrets and so did Kat. Demetry avoided his family, and so did Kat. Demetry's mother was difficult, and so was Kat's. He allowed her to stay with him whenever she felt the need to. She had her own bedroom and came and went as she pleased. Demetry didn't harass her and make accusations; Demetry was kind and gentle. He accepted her and was patient with her. If she were attracted to him, things would have been different. She would have married him.

She was attracted to women, so she thought. She and her partner Sam were having difficulties. Sam was finally out of the closet, but her family and friends were very supportive of her "outing." Kat, on the other hand, preferred to keep her sexual tendencies a secret. Sam didn't like her secrecy. Kat didn't like her bossy personality. Their relationship was off and on; Kat would break it off with her for short periods of time but somehow they always managed to get back together—Sam said she couldn't live without her. Kat thought about telling her parents about her sexual orientation, telling Lucy maybe, but when she thought about how her mother would react, she decided against it. Her parents were fed up with her, she knew. They'd like for her to settle down, get a job, and get an apartment maybe with some roommates. Sam volunteered to live with her, and Kat agreed, trying to explain to her that they could be roommates; her parents would never know the difference. But Sam argued that she was her lover, not her roommate.

Kat didn't like complication or high maintenance. Why did everything have to be so difficult? Sam was difficult....

Kat wasn't too sure what to do about Sam. She loved her but, some days she really couldn't be bothered. She liked to be free, do what she wanted.

Complicated. Everybody so complicated.

CHAPTER 14

Thomas

"Hey Tommy? Who's your sister's friend, the one we picked up today from the dress shop?"

Tommy and Charles sat at the local coffee shop, drinking their lattes and checking out the waitresses.

"Never mind Charles, she's a bit too young for you. Hey! I missed you, man. Neighborhood was never the same without you." Tommy pushed Charles in the arm.

"Yeah? Well, life's been a little harsh to me, man." Charles looked down at his hands. "Your sister Lucy, she doesn't forget anything, does she?"

"I'm not sure what you mean."

"Never mind. Her friend, what was her name? Amelia? She is sweet!"

Tommy's face turned red and flushed. "Let's change the subject. I told you, she's too young for you. Why don't you tell me what you've been doing with yourself these last few years?" Tommy tried to remain calm. He knew his anger was unwarranted.

"Are you writing a book or something?" Charles asked.

"Not quite, but it would probably be a bestseller."

They both laughed.

"Honestly, Tommy, it's no big deal. After my mother died, they tried to put me in foster care. Can you believe that? *Foster* care." Charles leaned into the table and banged his fists down aggressively.

"Yeah, that's rough, man." He looked down at his coffee.

"Those jerks didn't know me. They had no idea who they were messing with." Charles stopped to light himself a smoke. "So, I left town on my motorbike. Drove all the way south until I hit Maryland. Got hitched up with a few local fishermen, and that was the end of it. I worked from boat to boat. I usually slept at a buddy's house or on the boats if the owners would let me. It was cool, man. Met a lot of nice people, but it wasn't exactly home sweet home. I moved around a lot."

94

Tommy looked at Charles. He looked tired. His face looked weathered and aged from the sun and wind. He had lines around his eyes, probably from the stress of being on his own. "Someday I'll own my own boat, Tommy. That's where the money is. You should come in on it with me. Help me buy a boat!" Charles exclaimed with enthusiasm.

"Yeah, that sounds cool Charles, but I'm happy at Boston College. Got a full four-year baseball scholarship."

"Oh yeah? Yeah, that's great, Tommy. You've always wanted that. I'm happy for you."

"Thanks, man. So, what brings you back to Connecticut?"

"Honestly, I was hoping Jack would be here," Charles answered quietly. Hoping he comes back when he turns eighteen. I wanted to be here if he does."

"You haven't heard from Jack at all?"

"No, I haven't." Charles' gaze was fixed on the drink before him. He was unable to look Tommy in the eyes. "I left him, Tommy. I'll never forgive myself."

"You boys were kids," Tommy said, trying to console him. "You didn't know."

"Yeah, I guess." Charles leaned back in his chair. "Anyway, I hear your sister Kathryn has herself quite the hookup. I've been trying to reach her so I can score some weed."

"What? What the hell are you talking about?"

"You know, she has connections!"

Tommy shook his head. "I don't know."

"Oh, okay, sorry. Well, hey, I got to split, Tommy. I'll have to catch up with you again, brother. It's been nice." Charles left the coffee bar and walked down the street toward the not-so-nice part of town.

Tommy watched Charles as he left the building. He grabbed his coat and hurriedly made his exit, his expression visibly worried. What the hell was Kathryn up to? He let out an exhausted sigh. *Why do I always have to worry about all these girls? Stupid...so stupid!* And *Amelia.* Tommy forgot about her. He needed to call her, give her a heads-up about Charles. Make sure she kept her distance.

Amelia...why did she have to be so cute...so infectious...so beautiful?

CHAPTER 15

Thomas

The phone rang and rang. *Pick up, pick up.* Nothing. Thomas slammed the phone down. Quickly, he picked up the phone again and dialed her number. *Dammit! Pick up the phone.*

"Hello?" she answered.

"Amelia, it's me!"

"Oh! Hello you!" She giggled.

"Stop it, Amelia. It's important. Can you meet me? At our spot?"

"Yeah, I guess I can. Sure. When?"

"Now!"

"Ugh, you're so bossy!"

"I'll be by in ten minutes to pick you up. Be ready!"

Thomas jumped into his car and quickly drove down the street toward Amelia's mother's house. He thought about Amelia and the innocent affect she had on people. She was stunning to look at and so pure, the way she genuinely smiled at people. The affect she had on him made him crazy. Her personality was charming and intelligent, funny and entertaining. She was a special person. Thomas had never met anyone like her, and he doubted that he ever would.

Thomas' heart was beating rapidly with anticipation. These meetings with Amelia were few and far in between, and he looked forward to them, waited for them. He pulled his vehicle up alongside her, then opened the door and told her to jump in.

"Hey baby," Amelia said. Thomas leaned over and kissed her lightly on her lips. He drove down the street to a dead end road and parked under a large oak tree. Thomas shut off the car, turned, and faced Amelia. He pulled her toward him into a tight embrace.

"I've been waiting all week to hold you, Amelia. This is so hard. I need you. I need to see you, every day," Tommy whined. He grabbed her face and kissed her softly. "You drive me crazy," Thomas whispered. Amelia wrapped her hands around Tommy's neck and leaned in closer, rubbing her chest against his.

"You know how I feel, Tommy. You drive me just as crazy."

Thomas pulled Amelia up onto his lap so she could straddle him. He grabbed her ass tightly and buried his face into her chest. She smelled so good, so sweet. They held each other. He kissed her chest, her neck, and her face. He kissed her lips, slowly pulling at her, sticking his tongue in her mouth. Amelia moaned. She rubbed her thighs against his hips, urging him on so she could feel his manhood, so stiff and strong.

"Please Tommy. I need you," she said breathlessly.

Thomas groaned. There was nothing more he wanted than to feel her insides. Feel her virginity slipping away while he took it from her.

"I want you so bad, Amelia. You feel so damn good," Thomas panted.

Amelia took Tommy's hand and rubbed it against her sweet spot.

"God, you're so wet," he uttered beneath his breath. Thomas slipped off her underwear. He grabbed her face and held it between both of his hands. He looked into her eyes. "Are you sure about this, Amelia? Are you really sure?"

"I'm ready, Tommy. I've never been more sure. I love you. I want this." She smiled down at him.

Tommy pulled off his pants and sat Amelia on top of him. He slowly entered himself into her body.

"Oh my god, Amelia. You're incredible," he moaned.

A look of discomfort ripped across Amelia's face as Thomas began to enter her deeper. "Go slow, Thomas, go slow," she whispered.

"Are you okay? Am I hurting you?" Tommy asked, concerned.

Amelia closed her eyes. "It hurts, but it's okay. Keep going."

Tommy rocked her slowly, back and forth, and watched her face. She began to moan quietly and joined him in rhythm while they rocked each other, holding each other tightly. "I can't hold back much longer, Amelia," Tommy grunted.

"It's okay, Tommy, I'm ready," she said in his ear. Tommy grabbed Amelia's ass and shoved himself deeper, with a sharp thrust, again and again.

"Oh god!" Amelia yelled. "Do it quickly!" Amelia's body stiffened from the sharp pain and soreness of losing her virginity. Tommy let himself go, enjoying his orgasm but feeling guilty over the discomfort he had caused her.

Satisfied, they both collapsed into each other, taking deep breaths, hearts pounding.

Amelia lifted her head off Tommy's chest and looked into his face. She smiled widely.

"That was awesome!" She giggled.

"That was fantastic," Tommy agreed. He kissed her nose. "I will never get enough of you Amelia and I promise, it only gets better."

Amelia dragged herself off Thomas and sat next to him on the car seat. They both dressed and straightened themselves out.

"What if a car came by?" Amelia asked, laughing.

"I know, right?"

"So, this is why you dragged me out of my house, so desperate to see me, Tommy? So, we can *do* it?" Amelia teased.

Tommy's smile faded; he almost forgot why he wanted to see her.

"No, Amelia. That wasn't at all what I expected. I wanted to warn you," he stated seriously.

"Warn me, why?"

"You know that guy I was with today, Charles?"

"Yes."

"Well, he has taken quite an interest in you. He was asking me lots of questions about you."

"Oh, so you wanted to see me because you're jealous?" Amelia asked again, trailing her finger along his ear, teasing him.

"Well, no...I mean, yes...well no...." He sighed. "I'm just worried, I guess," Tommy responded, feeling silly about his insecurity.

Amelia looked at him seriously. "I don't have any interest in anyone but you, Tommy. Lots of guys have an interest in me. You're the only one."

"I'm not jealous. I don't trust the guy. I want you to be careful, that's all." Tommy held onto her hand.

"I'm always careful! I'm more worried about Lucy. I'm worried what she'll say when she finds out we're together. What are we going to tell her?" Concern shone out from her eyes.

"It's none of her business anyway; who cares?"

"She's my best friend. I don't want to hurt her."

"Yeah, well, she doesn't need to know, Amelia. Let's just keep this a secret for now. You're so special to me. I don't want to spoil it." Tommy kissed her face.

"Okay, Tommy," Amelia said as she put her hand in his hair. "I should head back now, but I want to walk. I want to think about what we just did. Remember it, again and again." Amelia smiled and winked at Tommy. Tommy was always surprised and delighted by her confidence. What did he just get himself into? She made him lose all thoughts and sensibilities. He couldn't control his feelings when he was around her.

"I'll call you tomorrow." Tommy grabbed her arm before she could leave. "Amelia, I...I love you," he said as he kissed her gently, softly covering her cheeks and lips.

Amelia chuckled. "I love you too, Tommy. See you tomorrow!"

Tommy watched Amelia walk down the road toward her street. She practically skipped down the road, occasionally looking back at Thomas.

"Trouble," Thomas stated out loud. "Nothing but trouble!"

CHAPTER 16

Mama

"Michael Anthony! Get your butt upstairs right now, and clean up the urine that is all around the toilet seat. *Right now!*" Mama sighed. "What the hell is wrong with that kid? He can't even pee in the toilet."

"Mom, you do it! You clean it yourself!"

"No Mikey, you need to learn how to use the toilet properly. There are other people living in this house! There is no reason for this! If you don't get up here, I'm going to tell your father. Try harder not to miss next time. Don't be in such a hurry and don't be such a slob!"

"You're the worsest!" Mikey yelled from the stairway.

Mama took a deep breath. She was really trying to remain calm. Trying to keep it all together. Her younger children were exhausting. Her older children were disappearing and moving on with their lives. She didn't have control anymore, and her husband, he just worked and worked. There was no end to this life. She felt so overwhelmed. There was so much anxiety.

Where's my calendar? What day is it? Tuesday! Kaylan had band practice after school. Jessica would be at dance until 4:00. Julia would be coming home this weekend. She needed to talk to her about Kathryn. What was going on with her? Maybe Julia and Lucy would have some idea. Maybe Tommy. "Mikey, get your jacket on. We need to pick up the girls!" *Where are my car keys? Dinner, what about dinner?* "Lucy, honey? Can you keep an eye on Mikey? I need to pick up the girls."

"Yeah sure, Mom, no problem."

Lucy. What would she do without Lucy? She really was a savior.

CHAPTER 17

Lucy

"Hey Mikey. Come with me, I want to show you something."

Mikey complained weakly but continued to follow me up the stairs to his bedroom.

"I'm so glad I didn't have to go with Mama," he murmured, grinning.

"What's the matter, you don't want to sit in a car and wait for Kaylan and Jessica to be picked up from their after-school activities?" I glanced quickly at Mikey and threw him a mischievous smile. Mikey was in sixth grade now; he was growing up and starting to catch on to things.

"Lucy, have you driven with Mama lately? It's not fun, it's almost scary!"

I had noticed Mama's parking in the driveway lately. It was as if she needed glasses. She either parked half on, half off the driveway, or she was half in, half out. It was as if her brain couldn't make up its mind.

"Well, she's never been the best driver," I stated flippantly, not wanting to alarm Mikey any further. Mikey continued to roll his eyes at me as he leaned against his bedroom door. He was an extremely spoiled boy. I suppose being the youngest child, it's natural to become a little selfish and overindulged. We were all guilty of it, my sisters and I. Mikey was like a baby toy when he was born. There was quite a gap between us kids—six years between Mikey and I. I loved him to pieces; he was a special little boy, but what a pain in the ass when he wanted to be.

"What do you have, Lucy? Why did you call me up here?"

I smiled again at my eager little brother. I knew that what I was about to give him was going to blow his mind. He may think that I am the best person in the universe after this exchange.

"Sit down and close your eyes," I said playfully.

"Are you kidding me?" he asked, annoyed.

"Do it or forget it."

Mikey did what I asked of him. I reached down under his mattress and pulled out the two new *Spiderman* comic books that he'd been harassing my father about for weeks now.

"You can open your eyes now," I suggested sweetly.

Mikey opened his eyes and looked down at the comic books placed on his lap. His eyes went wide with disbelief, his smile, priceless.

"You got me these? These are for me, Lucy?" Mikey asked the questions, thumbing through the pages eagerly as if there were money stuffed in those pages, and all he had to do was find it.

"They are for you Mikey, enjoy them." I kissed him on the cheek.

"You're the best, Lucy. Thank you so much," Mikey said. He returned the sentiment of affection quickly.

"You're welcome. I need to start dinner. Call me if you need me."

"Yeah, sure. No problem. These will keep me busy for awhile."

I watched Mikey lean back on his pillow in his bed and I walked out of the room, satisfied with my moment of goodness.

I thought about starting dinner for Mama. Since Julia had left, my mother had been running ragged. Kathryn was no help. She was never around. Tommy was no help either. He was a boy and spent most of his time at school. Oh well, let's see, first I'll set the table. Mama was making sauce and it smelled so good. I could start the pasta for her and make a salad. "Are you okay up there, Mikey?" I yelled up the stairs.

"YYEEESSS!" he replied.

Good, I guess he's fine. Let me call Amelia while I'm stuck here in the kitchen. I could at least talk to her. I grabbed the phone but before I could dial, it began to ring.

"Hello," I answered.

"Hi Lucy. It's me!"

"Amelia, I was just going to pick up the phone and call you. That's so weird."

"It's not weird, we're connected, that's all," Amelia stated, laughing. "So, what are you doing?"

"Just helping with dinner, you?"

"I just got off the phone with Izzy. She wants to know if the three of us could do a sleepover after prom. What do you think, Lucy?"

"Oh, I don't care, Amelia. That's fine with me if you want to. Should be fun," I said happily. Izzy had that crazy dog that always liked to jump on me. *I'll have to remember to remind her that I don't want my dress ruined.*

"Well, her parents will be out of town, Lucy. Do you think your mom will let you sleep over if no one is home?"

"Umm, I'm not going to tell her that, duh!" I replied sarcastically. My mother would have a fit if she knew.

"Oh good."

"She won't bother checking either; she's really focused on the girls and Mikey lately. I don't think she's worried about what I'm doing. Besides, she trusts me."

"Well, as long as my mother knows I'm with you, she won't worry about me either."

"So, you're coming to my house Friday, before the dance?"

Oh god, my whole family would be here. Thomas too. I hope he doesn't embarrass me.

"Yes, Izzy's sister is dropping her off here, and then we'll come by to your house. Do you think Tommy can drive us to the dance? Have you asked him?"

"I haven't yet, but I will. If not, my dad will."

"I'm so excited, Lucy. It's going to be so fun."

Where the hell does my mother keep the pasta? I thought to myself as I talked with Amelia. "Hey Amelia, can I call you later? I have to do something and I can't talk and cook at the same time!" I made Amelia laugh.

"What's wrong with you? Can't talk and cook. You're crazy, Lucy! Call me later!"

"Bye bye, then!" I hung up the phone and headed back to the cabinet. No pasta. I looked in the pantry. No pasta. *Where does she keep the pasta?* I continued to open every drawer. Finally, pasta!

I heard my mother's car pull up in the driveway. She walked into the house with Kaylan.

"Hey Kay," I said. "Hi Mom, I started dinner. Mom, why is there pasta in this drawer and yogurt in this cabinet?" I asked as I pointed around the kitchen.

"What?" My mom looked at me like I was speaking Chinese.

"Mom, where's Jessica?" I asked.

"Mama didn't pick her up," Kay said casually.

"Why?" I asked, startled, looking at my mother.

"Oh my god! Jessica!" My mother grabbed her bag and keys. She ran for the door. "Be right back, girls." I stopped and stared at the front door and listened to my mother's car as she peeled out of the driveway. How did she forget Jessica? I looked over at Kaylan with a confused look on my face as Kaylan stood there, equally confused and disgusted.

"Mom's weird," Kaylan said. "She's forgetting everything, Lucy. She forgot to put lunch in my lunch bag today. It was empty. She gave me an empty lunchbox!"

"You must be starving. Do you want a snack?"

"No, I'm okay. My friend shared her lunch with me. Her mother always over-packs her lunch." Kaylan jumped off the chair. "I opened it, and it was just empty!" Kaylan shook her head back and forth.

My poor mother, she's got too much on her mind. She's always distracted, worried. I'll try to talk to her after dinner, see if she needs more help from me.

Thomas walked into the kitchen, the usual look of hunger spread across his face. "What's for dinner, Luce?" he asked as he dropped his backpack onto the counter.

"Mama made sauce and I'm cooking the pasta now. Should be ready in ten minutes," I answered.

"Good. I'm hungry!"

I laughed as I continued to prepare dinner. "What else is new? You're *always* hungry!" I turned to look at him. "Hey, Tommy? Can you drive us to the prom on Friday night?" I asked timidly. I was still a little uneasy around Tommy, never really sure if he was going to be in a good mood, or a bad one.

"Who's 'us'?"

"Amelia, Izzy, and I. The prom is at the high school. Please, Tommy? I don't want to ask Dad. He'll be a drag."

"No problem, Lucy. I'll take you girls. Be happy to!"

"Oh my gosh. Thank you so much, Tommy. I really appreciate it," I said with gratitude.

"What time do you think?"

"Probably six. I know Amelia likes to make an entrance. Wait till all the boys get a look at her in her dress. She's stunning, absolutely stunning. I'm really excited."

"Let me know when supper's ready, Lucy. I'll be in my room." Thomas turned to leave the kitchen.

"Sure Tommy." I chuckled to myself as Thomas cleared the room and I began to set the table. I could hear my father's car door slam and I was thankful that he was home before my mother. Maybe I could talk to him before she got back and get his perspective on the situation.

"Hi Dad!" I said cheerfully as my father walked through the front door.

"Hi honey. How are you?"

I reached up and hugged my father.

"Not too close honey, I need to shower…"

"Hey Dad, have you noticed anything weird about Mom lately, like she's really forgetful?" I asked.

"Your mother has a million thoughts a day, honey. We all get forgetful."

"I know, but she forgot to pick up Jessica today from dance. She came home without her!" I said, concerned.

"Did she really?" My father started to laugh. "Oh, I'm not going to let her forget that one. No way."

"Dad, it's not funny!"

"It's okay, honey; don't worry about your mother. Its a part of growing old and a result of having too many children!"

"Yeah, I guess so," I replied, not really convinced. Did having too many children mean you left spoiled food in the cupboard? Something more was happening here.

"I'm going to shower. I'll be down shortly and we can all eat dinner."

"Okay, Dad," I said. *I guess I'll go through some of these cabinets real quick and put things back to where I think they belong. That will help her...I hope.*

CHAPTER 18

Kathryn

Kathryn decided she definitely wouldn't be making it home for dinner tonight. It was disappointing because she wanted to spend some time with her family. She just got a call from Charles, an old neighborhood friend of hers. He wanted to hang out and visit. He also wanted to make a purchase from her. Demetry grew some of the best marijuana available in town. He grew it and she sold it. Demetry didn't like to get out into public that much—you could say he was a little bit of a hermit—so she needed to stick around tonight if she wanted to make any sort of money. She needed to make herself available with this type of job. Her customers called her at all hours of the day. It made her life a little inconvenient, but it was better than working a real nine-to-five job.

She told Sam that she was going home tonight to be with her family. It was a convenient excuse because Sam had never met her family. Sam wouldn't dare call her house either. She knew that would be crossing the line. Anyway, what would she say?

Kathryn told Charles she'd meet him at The Tavern downtown. She was actually looking forward to it. Charles was always a wild child; he lived a little on the edge. It'll be good to catch up, see what'd become of him.

"Hey Demetry? Can you give me a lift downtown, to The Tavern?" She looked at Demetry. He was lying on the couch, reading a *Horticulture* magazine. He glanced at her, over his paper.

"Where're you going, girl?"

"I need to meet a customer," she said.

"You need to get yourself a car."

"Why should I get a car, when I've got you to drive me places?" she asked him with her hand on her hip.

"Yeah well, it's annoying. I have a life, you know."

"Umm, you do? Seems to me like all you do is stare at your plants in the basement, smoke pot, and gaze at the wall." She laughed as he rolled his eyes at her. He really didn't have any kind of life.

Demetry grew up in her neighborhood, one street over from her house. Kat met him through his younger sister, who was about her age. They'd been friends for years and now, she pretty much lived at his house. He knew about Sam. She told him everything. He was the only one she trusted. He accepted her for who she was—a lesbian—and she accepted him—a small-time, recluse pot dealer. "Please, Dem?" she begged.

"Yeah, I guess so. You need the money and I need to move this weed!" He dragged himself off the couch.

"It's good, Dem, it's really good. You grow exceptional drugs."

"Are you staying here tonight, or will you be going home?"

"Not sure, just leave the door open, I might be back."

"Alright, let's go then. Get you out of my hair."

"Dem, you love this!" she stated as they walked out of the house.

Dem started to laugh. "No, I don't love this."

They headed down the road toward town and began to pass through the stoplights on Main Street. Ten lights to be exact—one after another, stop and go until you eventually reached your destination. Each light would represent an intersection of a major street or development, a CVS, or a local

118

gas station on every corner. Dem eventually pulled up to the bar situated on the first level of a multi-apartment building located on the west side of town. Not the best area to meet up with an old friend, but it was close to Charles' apartment, so it was convenient for him.

"Do you want to come in? Have a drink with us?" she asked, not sure how comfortable she was to be alone with Charles.

"No thanks. I've got some calls to make. Be careful, Kat," he said caringly.

She opened the door to get out of the car. "Okay, Dem. I'll see you later. Thanks a lot."

"Hey, smartass? Don't forget your drugs." Dem threw her a dime bag.

"Ugh, I'm really bad at this job," she said as she made the catch.

She walked into the bar and looked around. She didn't notice Charles at first; he looked so different. He looked beat-up, tired. He waved her down; she guessed she must look the same. "Hi Charles. How are you?"

"Wow Kathryn, you look fantastic. You haven't changed a bit," Charles stated kindly.

"Thanks Charles. You look like hell."

Charles smiled. "You were always the honest one, Kathryn. You never held anything back."

"It's great to see you," she said as they embraced.

"Are you hungry?"

"No, I just ate. Thank you. Could really use a drink, though."

"Me too. What can I get you?" Charles asked.

"I'll take a beer. Sounds good right about now."

"Bartender! Two bud drafts please," Charles ordered.

Charles motioned her to the other side of the room. "Do you want to sit at a booth?"

"Sure," she said. They walked awkwardly across the room to the booths. It was a slow night, just a few locals sitting at the bar.

"I'm going to hit up the jukebox, Kathryn. Anything special you want to hear?"

"They have a good mix of music. Surprise me," she said. The bartender brought them their beers and placed them carefully on the table. Charles lingered at the jukebox for a minute. Finally, some music came on. Janice Joplin. "Good choice, Charles," she said with a smile.

"Yeah, you like her?"

"I like all kind of music. I love to go to concerts."

"Me too. I hear the Foo Fighters are coming to town next month. Maybe we could go?"

"Sure," she said. She sipped on her beer.

Charles sat across from her.

"Oh, I almost forgot." Kat slid the bag across the table. Charles picked it up quickly. He then slid his money back across the table to her. She grabbed it and put it in her pocket.

"Thanks, Kathryn. This helps kill the boredom I'm dying from being back here in this town."

"It's not that bad, Charles."

"It's bad when you've been other places, seen other things."

"Why did you come back then?"

"I was hoping to find Jack, my brother. My guess is that he went out west with our grandfather. I tried to contact the social worker and the police officer that was handling our case. The police officer has retired and no one seems to know who Mrs. Nelson is. I don't know how to find him. I'm not even sure what my grandfather's name is."

"That's terrible," she replied, feeling his frustration.

"I know. It's killing me. I thought maybe when he turned eighteen, he'll come back here."

"Yeah, maybe, although he doesn't have great memories of this place," she added.

"I know. I don't even want to be here. Why would he want to be here?"

"Well, you can always leave your phone number with someone like me or like your neighbors, maybe my mother. That way if Jack does come back, we could tell him how to reach you. That you've been looking for him," she suggested.

"That's a great idea, Kathryn, although I plan to stick around here for a minute. I just got a job working at the steel factory downtown and I rented a small apartment. It feels kind of good to be around some old familiar faces and to be on solid ground. I've been living on a boat for years now."

"Just thinking of a boat makes me feel seasick," she said.

"I love being on a boat. I eventually want to own my own boat and become a commercial fisherman."

"That's great Charles. It's good to have goals, so I'm told." She chuckled.

"You have goals, Kathryn. I'm sure you don't want to sell weed your whole life."

"Yeah, I guess not. I don't know what I want to do. It's really hard to figure it out."

"You need to travel, Kathryn. Experience different places. You're stuck here. Your choices are limited. Hey, do you want another beer?"

"Sure!" she said, enjoying herself. Kathryn was surprised at how much Charles' encouragement affected her, how his positive words enlightened her, perhaps even motivated her.

"Bartender!" Charles waved to the bartender for another round.

"Where would I go? I have nowhere to go," she said.

"You'll figure it out, Kathryn."

She smiled at him. He was rough around the edges but he'd been places. He took a hard road and he was still standing.

"Cheers, Charles," she said as she picked up her mug and they clanked them together.

"Cheers."

"To goals!" Kat laughed.

"Yeah! To figuring it out!"

CHAPTER 19

Jack

Pop registered me for senior year at high school against my better judgment. The last few years Susie Mae has homeschooled me, my refusal to attend public school strong and effective. Pop said he would love to keep me home with him again, to work on the farm. He also said it would do me good to meet more people and make new friends. I would rather stay on the farm and work with Pop and the fellas. Help Susie with the chickens. I was almost eighteen and not really interested in going to high school at this point. I knew what I was going to do with my life. I knew that I would work the farm until the day I died.

"Are you going to sit on your bed all day, Jack?"

"No, Pop. Just trying to gather some strength and will to bring myself to school."

Pop sat down on the bed next to me. "You'll do fine, Jack. It's important for you to finish your schooling. The farm will be here when you get out. It's not going anywhere."

"It seems like a huge waste of time, Pop."

"I know, I know. Come on, buddy. You can take the truck. She'll get you to class and back."

"Yeah, Pop?" I asked.

"Yeah, why not."

I took the truck keys from Pop and went outside. Susie stood waiting for me, a lunch bag in her hand. "Here you go, Jack. I made your favorite."

I stopped and bent down to kiss Susie on the cheek. "Thank you. You know I love your egg salad," I said.

"I know it, Jack," she replied with a smile.

I hopped into the truck and headed for town. I waved as I pulled out of the driveway. I felt anxious. I've always had Charles with me at every corner of my life. I've never had to make friends before and although I've met some nice people here, they never seemed to make me feel comfortable. I still felt that I didn't quite fit in here. Charles has always paved the way for me. He made my life easy. Maybe this school year would be different.

I pulled into the parking lot of the high school. I sat in my truck and looked around at the crowd of students, waiting for the bell to ring. I made my way to the front office. An elderly woman was standing behind the desk. "Hello, son," she said as I approached her.

"Hi. My name is Jack Nimchak. I'm a senior here. I'm new."

"Just give me a second. Let me find you a schedule and figure out where you belong." She searched frantically on her desk for her glasses. "Okay. Yes, Jack. Here it is." The secretary put her reading glasses on so she could see the computer screen. "You belong in classroom A-3, Mrs. K's room. Go straight down the hall and take a left. Her classroom is on the right, can't miss it," she said as she pointed the direction I was supposed to go.

"Thank you, ma'am," I said kindly.

"You welcome, and good luck dear."

I left the office and headed to room A-3. I knocked on the door and let myself in. Everyone was staring at me. "Hello, my name is Jack. I'm told this is my classroom," I said nervously.

"Hello Jack. I am Mrs. K. I've been expecting you, welcome," she said.

"Thank you."

"You can take a seat at any empty chair. We were just taking attendance."

I looked around. This was a small class with plenty of empty seats. I choose to sit in the back row. A few faces turned to say hello to me. This wasn't so bad, I thought to myself. I recognized a few students from Sunday Mass at the congregational church. "Adam, would you be so kind as to show Jack around the school? Show him the cafeteria, his locker and where his next class will be?"

"Sure, Mrs. K.," Adam replied.

Adam and I stood and I followed him to the door. We started to walk down the hallway together.

"Hey Jack." Adam reached out his hand to shake mine.

"Hi Adam," I said duplicating the gesture.

"It's nice to meet some new faces around this school. It gets pretty boring around here," Adam stated.

"Yeah, I guess."

"Where are you from?"

"Connecticut. I moved out here a few years back to stay with my grandfather. He owns Green Acres Farm off of Chamberland Highway," I answered.

"Oh yeah? I know that farm. My parents used to bring my sister and I up there to pick apples in the orchard. Nice farm!" Adam replied with enthusiasm. "Boy you're a far way from Connecticut," he added.

"Yeah, " I said, losing interest in the small talk.

"What brought you out west?"

"It's a long story. I don't really want to get into it," I said.

"Sure, no problem. Here's the senior cafeteria. Did you bring lunch or will you be buying lunch?" Adam asked.

"I've brought a lunch," I answered.

"Good choice. The food here is double thumbs down." Adam made the gesture with his hands.

I smiled. "I didn't know people still used that expression."

"Well, I can say other things about the school cafeteria food, but I'm trying to be polite." He laughed.

"Okay so, bring lunch every day. Got it!"

"God, the girls are going to go crazy for you," Adam said enviously.

"Huh?" I looked at him confused.

"You're a senior, you're big and strong, obviously, and you're good looking. *Not that I'm into that kind of thing.* Just saying. We need to hang out!"

I laughed. "Well, you're officially my first and only friend, Adam, so…no problem! We can hang out," I said sarcastically.

"Great. Hey, I'll meet you after class. We'll have lunch together."

"Okay. Sounds good. See you later." Adam turned and left. I walked to my next class. I thought about Charles. Charles would have hated Adam. I smiled and shook my head.

CHAPTER 20

Lucy

I *loved* my dress. It fit me perfectly. The cream-colored dress with its pleats and lace was even prettier than I remembered it. The flowing material flattered my waist and its fitted bodice exploited my curves in all the right places. I couldn't believe it was the day of the prom.

"Mom, can you help me zip my dress?" I asked.

"Be right there, honey."

I moved around my bedroom, looking for my shoes. I put them on and started walking in them. I needed to stretch them out a bit. I started playing with my hair. I felt a little anxious. My mother walked into the room, eager to help me.

"Mama, should I wear my hair up or down?" I turned to let her zip up my dress.

"Oh, I think up. You look so grown; let me take a look at you, Lucy. You're beautiful."

"Thank you, Mama. Do you really think so?"

"Absolutely! This dress is perfect on you. You're really quite stunning," Mama said with a smile.

"So, after the dance we are going to head to Izzy's house and we'll be sleeping over," I reminded her casually.

"What, wait a minute? You didn't tell me this," my mom stated, annoyed.

"Yes I did, Mom. I asked you a few days ago. You said it was fine."

My mother took a deep breath. "Lucy, I would rather you come home. I'm tired and I don't want to worry about you all night. I just want you home, in your own bed."

"*Mom!* I already made the plans, this isn't fair!"

"You can change them. Now, don't get all upset about it. My mind is made up. You still have the dance and it will still be fun, okay?"

I stood looking at my mother in absolute shock. This was going to ruin everything. Amelia would be totally upset if I couldn't go to Izzy's.

"Mom, please. The girls are expecting me."

"Sorry, Lucy. The answer is no. Do you want me to help you with your hair?" my mother asked.

"No, I don't!" I couldn't believe she was ruining my night. *I'll never forgive her for this*, I thought. "I'm all set, Mama, you can go. Let me know when Amelia gets here."

"Okay, dear. Call me if you need me." My mother left my room and I sat on my bed.

How could she do this? She said yes just two days ago; I don't understand. Maybe I'll talk to my father. What am I going to do, this sucks!

I heard Amelia's mother's car doors shut. Amelia's mom was very young; she had Amelia when she was in high school. I could hear my mother as she graciously talked with them, and Jessica screeching excitedly over Amelia and Izzy's dresses. She loved fashion and dress up. I imagined that she was inspecting Amelia's dress, lifting her skirt and touching the material. I smiled at the thought of all the attention my siblings were giving my friends. I took one last look at myself in the mirror and decided I better head downstairs and save them.

As I walked down the stairs, Kaylan saw me first. "LUCY!" she yelled. "Wow!"

"Thank you, Kaylan. That's the kind of response I'm hoping to get from everybody." I giggled.

"You look so pretty," Jessica said.

"Wow, you girls look fantastic," my mother added. I smiled at Izzy and Amelia. I could barely look at my mother.

"I just love that dress on you, Lucy. I'm so glad I made you try it on," Amelia said proudly.

"Me too, Amelia. I would have never picked this for myself." I turned and looked at Izzy. "Iz, your hair is totally cool."

Izzy smiled. "I know. My big sister did it for me. She's really talented. She wants to be a hairdresser."

"You look beautiful," I said. "Do you think I should put my hair up?" I asked everyone.

"No, Lucy!" Amelia stated. "Your hair is beautiful! It's long and wavy. It's perfect with your dress."

"You think?" I asked, uncertain.

"Yes, absolutely."

My mother grabbed her camera. "Get together, girls. I need to take a picture."

We all squished together, awkward and happy. My mother snapped about a hundred pictures. I heard another car door shut. It must be Tommy.

"I think Tommy's here." I needed to check my makeup one more time. I quickly glanced at myself in the mirror hanging in the hallway. When I turned around, I could see Tommy as he walked through the door. He was floored when he saw Amelia. He was such a dope. When was he going to stop gawking at her, I thought to myself.

"Wow ladies. Wow!" Thomas exclaimed. I could see Amelia's face turn red as she started to blush.

"Hi Tommy," she responded softly.

"Hi Tommy." Izzy waved.

"Tommy, get in between the two girls so I can take a picture." My mother positioned herself in front of the threesome and readied herself to snap more pictures.

Tommy reluctantly got in between my two girlfriends. You could tell he was happy to be near Amelia, but he always hated to have his picture taken. He'd given my mother a hard time about pictures ever since he was three years old.

My mother took the picture. I would look at this picture later on in life and smile, Amelia looking up at Tommy. She was so happy, a huge cheesy smile on her face.

Satisfied with my appearance but very careful in my heels, I walked around my mother and joined my friends for the picture. Tommy looked at me.

"Gee Lucy, who knew you were so pretty? You hide it well," he said teasingly.

"Shut up, Tommy!"

"I'm just kidding, you look great. Are you ladies ready?"

"Yes," we replied in unison.

"Let's go then." Tommy held the door for us as we made a mass exodus out of the kitchen and onto the front lawn. Tommy must have worked all day cleaning his car for us. It was sparkling and gleaming with newly Armor Alled wheels and Windexed windows. His old Chevy Nova was neatly restored and cool and I was happy to be riding in it.

"Wow Tommy, the car looks great!" Amelia said.

"I didn't want you girls to get your dresses dirty. Besides, it needed a good cleaning." Tommy looked and smiled at Amelia. She couldn't take her eyes off him.

"Can I sit in the front?" Amelia asked, knowing damn well what the answer to that question was.

"Lucy, you and Izzy can sit in the back," Thomas stated. I was too busy talking to Izzy to notice anything unusual. We all got in the car and waved at our mothers and my sisters as we pulled out of the driveway.

"Goodbye, girls, have fun!" my mother yelled.

I sat in the back seat and waved and then turned to Izzy. I quietly told her that I couldn't stay at her house after the dance. I told her that my mother wanted me home. Amelia turned in her seat to look at me with a crushed look on her face.

"What? You're not coming?"

"No. I can't, Amelia. My mother says she doesn't remember me asking her for permission. She wasn't happy about it and she wants me home," I whined.

"Oh no! That's terrible."

Tommy grabbed Amelia's arm and pulled her back into her seat. "Sit down, Amelia."

She reluctantly sat down.

"Well, I can pick you girls up and drop you off wherever you need to be." He looked over at Amelia and winked.

"Thanks, Tommy. That would be great," I said.

"That sounds perfect!" Amelia said cheerfully.

Tommy pulled up the long, winding road to the high school. He jumped out of the car to open Amelia's door first. He bent down to whisper in her ear. She grinned then nodded her head slyly.

Tommy smiled. He opened the back door for me. I looked at the two of them.

"What was that all about?" I asked.

"Nothing. Just thanking Tommy for dropping us off," Amelia said dismissingly. Amelia grabbed my hand and pulled me away from the car.

"Come on, Izzy," she yelled. "Let's get inside. I can't wait to see the decorations!"

I smiled, suddenly feeling very excited. We've been planning this night for two months now; I couldn't believe it was finally here.

"I can't wait to see what everyone is wearing," Izzy said.

The three of us made our way to the school gym. We turned back and waved to Tommy. He remained leaning on his car with his arms folded watching us as we walked into the building.

"Ugh, he's so weird," I said.

"Stop it, Lucy. He's very nice to you. I don't know why he irritates you so much," Amelia said, defending him.

"Amelia, you wouldn't say so if you had to live with him." I rolled my eyes, disgusted.

We walked into the school gym and we were amazed at how beautiful the decorations were. "Boy, the prom committee did an awesome job," I said.

"Yeah, my older sister and her girlfriends are on the committee. They worked very hard to put this together," Izzy said proudly.

"Isn't it beautiful, girls?" Amelia asked. As I suspected, every boy in the room had their eyes on Amelia. She giggled and flirted with some of them, but she quickly announced to us that she didn't want to dance with anyone tonight.

"Amelia, you have to dance with someone," I harassed her. "Give some poor guy a chance," I teased.

Amelia laughed. "They're all boys, Lucy. I really have no interest," she stated flippantly.

"Okay, suit yourself," I said with a shrug.

"Besides, I don't see you dancing with anyone," Amelia retorted.

"Here comes Danny, Lucy. He definitely likes you," Izzy said, nudging me.

"What do I say if he wants to dance?" I asked, suddenly nervous.

"You say yes. He's so cute, Lucy, " Amelia said quietly.

"Hi, ladies. You all look lovely tonight," Danny said, greeting us with a short bow. We all giggled. "Lucy, would you care to dance with me?"

"Sure, Danny. Why not?"

Danny held out his hand to grab mine. Together we moved to the dance floor. I looked back at Amelia and Izzy. They were watching our every move. It was a slow dance, thank goodness. I put my arms around Danny's neck and he put his arms around my waist. I could tell he was very nervous. He looked at me and told me I looked pretty. Then he glanced away, unsure what else to say. We danced for a few minutes.

I started to think about Jack. Would he ask me to dance with him? Would he look me in the eyes, the way he did? Jack was never uncomfortable around me. I wondered what he was doing now, what he looked like, if he was happy. My heart always felt heavy when I thought of Jack. I wished I could have talked to him, one last time. I wished I could have said goodbye. His last words to me haunted me. I could never forget his voice, full of fear and sadness. The vulnerability, the way he cried in my arms the day I found him at his house, alone and lost. I wondered what would have happened between us. What would a real kiss be like now, now that we were older? I missed him. He was my friend.

Oh good, the music stopped.

"Gee Lucy, you looked like you were a million miles away," Danny stated.

"Sorry, I was just enjoying our dance. Thank you, Danny."

"Save another one for me later, Lucy!" He quickly walked off the dance floor, happy for the awkward encounter to be over with.

"Okay. I'll see you later." I walked back to Amelia. They were practically laughing themselves to death. "What's so funny?" I asked.

"Poor Danny, he didn't know what to do with you," Amelia said.

"Stop it, Amelia." I laughed. "It was very sweet," I added.

"Oh stop teasing her, Amelia," Izzy said.

"Thank you, Iz. I'm going to the restroom. I'll be right back," I stated, happy to get away.

"Okay," Amelia said. "Don't get lost."

I walked through the crowd to the restroom, thinking of Jack. I stared at myself in the mirror and put on my lipstick. I'd made up my mind. I wanted to find Jack. I needed to find Jack. There must be something I could do. I suddenly felt encouraged. If I could track down Charles, I'd make him tell me everything and then we could figure out a plan to find Jack. Yes, that's what I would do. Tomorrow. Tomorrow I'd find Charles.

CHAPTER 21

Mama

Mama tried eagerly to get her children to go to bed. She had such a headache. Lucy had looked beautiful tonight. She had grown into such a lovely young lady. When would she be home? Mama wanted the kids to go to bed so she could wait for her. She wanted to wait and see how her night was. She hoped Lucy would tell her everything. She wondered if she would dance with anyone. She really should be dating someone by now. She must have some interest in someone.

"Come on, Mikey," Mama said, pulling herself out of her daydream. "It's time for bed."

"Not yet, Mama, let me finish my game."

"Couple minutes, Mikey. Kaylan and Jessica! Let's go, it's time for bed." This day will never end. "Come on Kaylan, it's late, I don't want you up all night," she said as she pulled the blankets back off the pillows.

"Thank you, Mama." Kaylan smiled as she hopped into her bed.

"Mama?"

"Yes, Jessica."

"Can I wear Lucy's dress for my first dance?"

"Well, you would have to ask Lucy. I'm sure she wouldn't mind."

"Can you talk with us?" Jessica asked sweetly.

"Not tonight, girls. I want to wait for Lucy downstairs." She bent over and kissed them both. "Goodnight, girls."

"Good night, Mama."

"Come on, big boy. It's your turn," she said to Mikey as she grabbed a few items of clothing that were thrown on the floor.

"I hate bedtime!" It was the same routine, every night.

"I know, but you're a big boy now and it's important that you get the proper rest."

"I'm not even tired!"

"Don't give me a hard time, Mikey. Now kiss Mama goodnight."

"Good night, Mama."

"I love you, buddy."

"I love you too," he said sweetly. She shut the door quickly behind her and took a deep breath.

Finally, everyone was settled in, everyone except Lucy. When would she be home? Mama hated when she was out late.

"Hey, honey?" her husband asked as she walked into the kitchen. "Would you like a glass of wine?" Joseph was standing at the counter opening a bottle of merlot as he looked at her.

"No, thank you dear. I'm going to wait for Lucy. I don't want to be sleepy," she replied. He frowned at her. She wished she could relax and enjoy a glass of wine with her husband. She needed to wait for Lucy. That was all she could think about.

"Well, I think I'll take my drink upstairs then and watch the game, if you don't mind."

"No, that's fine. Go relax, honey." Her husband bent down to kiss her. She watched him as he walked up the stairs.

She waited until he was out of sight before she went to the door and looked outside the window. What time was it? It was 8:30. She'd be home soon. Maybe she shouldn't have let her go. What if something bad happened?

She prayed, "Dear Lord. Please look over my children tonight, keep them safe from harm and protect them always." She closed her eyes. Why couldn't she just relax? She sat and waited. These kids did so much more than she ever did. She never stayed out late. Her mother wouldn't allow it. Tommy would pick them up. He would keep them safe. Kids these days, they were faced with so much more. There was so much more danger. What if a drunk driver hits them as they drive home? She had such a headache. She needed to wash the sheets tomorrow. She needed to clean out Kaylan's closet. She sat and looked out the window.

She knew time was moving forward. She could feel her mind going numb as she gazed out into nothingness. She vaguely heard the noises around her. The clock ticking, the refrigerator running, and the wind against the windows were all faint sounds in comparison to her breathing. She sat in silence as she tried to focus her eyes, but she couldn't. She could gather her thoughts but she couldn't convey them to her body. She felt like she was sleeping, but she was awake.

She heard Joseph. He was pounding down the stairs like an elephant. Why was he so loud?

"Sweetheart, are you okay? It's 11:00. Have you've been sitting here this entire time? I thought you were watching TV?"

She looked at him bewildered and then looked at the clock, confused. She started to cry. "It's only been a few minutes. Why are you bothering me?"

"It's been hours, Sarah. Come on. Come with me. Lucy will be home soon. You need to lay down and get some rest."

"I'm not tired, Joe, I just want to wait. I just want the kids home safely." She started to sob. "Why can't you understand me? Why is this so difficult for you?" Her head was pounding and her hands started to shake.

"Settle down, honey. I'm just trying to help you. You're going to wake the children. I'm not trying to fight with you."

"Then leave me the FUCK alone!" she screeched.

"Okay…okay," Joseph said with his hands up.

"You don't know what it's like. You don't do ANYTHING for these kids. I do EVERYTHING. You don't care about us. You're a soul crusher! You're just like the devil! Get the hell away from me!"

Joseph stared at his wife in shock. "What is wrong with you?" he asked.

"Go FUCK yourself! I'm tired of this damn family! You wait for her then, asshole." She turned and walked out of the kitchen, up the stairs and into her room. She sat on the edge of her bed and sobbed. Her emotions were so out of control. She couldn't understand what was happening to her. Why was she so angry? She knew she was experiencing an episode. Her brain would shut off and she was unable to snap out of it.

What time was it? She needed to sleep. She would apologize in the morning. She was sorry for Joseph. She was so sorry. She was just tired. Where were her pills? She needed a sleeping pill. Here they were. She'll take one to help her sleep. She'll apologize in the morning. She didn't know what was wrong with her.

CHAPTER 22

Kathryn

Drinks with Charles turned out better than Kat expected. She asked him to drop her off at Dem's house. "Kat? We need to do this again," Charles said.

"Definitely," she said. She felt that stupid grin on her face.

"I'll look into that concert too. Are you still interested?" he asked.

"Yeah, I am." She smiled at Charles. He leaned into her to give her a kiss. She turned her head, not sure what to do. She gave him her cheek. "Thanks for the lift, Charles," she said as she exited the car.

"Yeah, no problem. I'll see you soon. I'll call you."

"Sounds good. See ya." She shut the door.

Dem left the lights on for her. He knew her so well. Charles beeped and drove off down the road. She watched him turn the corner and she thought about how nice her night was. She and Charles had a lot in common. He didn't make her feel like a disappointment or like a failure. He made her feel like she had a promising life ahead of her.

She opened the door to Dem's house and he was sitting at the kitchen table, a magazine still in his hand. "Reading?" she asked.

"Hey! I was waiting for you."

"Oh, well lucky for you I'm here and not at my parents' house. You would've been waiting for a long time," she said as she kissed him on the cheek.

"Yeah, lucky me!" Dem laughed sarcastically. "No, seriously though, Sam was here," he stated, suddenly very somberly.

"What?! She came here, why?"

"I don't know. She's looking for you."

"Well, what did you tell her?"

"I said that I thought you had mentioned going home to see your family. She didn't buy it."

"What the hell! She's so controlling. Can't I even get a drink with an old friend without her up my ass?"

"At least you were with a man and not a woman." Dem chuckled. "You need to talk to her, set her straight."

"I just want to go to bed," Kat whined.

"I thought you should know," he said as he stood up from his chair.

"Thanks. I'll see you in the morning."

"Hey, how was your date, by the way?"

"It wasn't a date Dem, but if you must know, it was nice. I like Charles. He's so easy to talk to."

"Good, I'm glad. Sam's no good for you, Kat."

"I know, Dem. It's so hard. I'm always so confused!"

Kat stomped out of the kitchen and into her room to sit on her bed. What was she going to tell her? What if she went by her house? Did she talk to her family? Who knows? She'll just tell her the truth. She'll be angry but she's not the boss of her. She's so exhausting.

Kat decided to take a shower and then go to bed. She undressed herself and turned on the water. She started to think about Charles. He was so laid back, so easygoing. She was impressed with the type of life he'd made for himself. How he took care of himself without any parents or family. Charles had a strength that she envied.

She'd never been with a man before. She'd never been with anyone other than Sam. She liked men. Charles was so sweet, trying to kiss her. She hoped she didn't make him feel weird. She had always been so curious about men. Sam just made it so hard to resist her. She was so bold and forward. Being with Sam was exciting at first. They were very secretive, obsessed with each other. Over time their relationship had become more of a burden. They'd been together for three years now and Kat thought she was ready to move on. She felt confused with her sexuality; she wasn't ready to commit to Sam and spend the rest of her life with her. She felt that if she questioned their relationship, perhaps then it was time that she should try to date other people—date a man, for instance—and see how that goes, see how she feels about that. But how would she tell her?

Dem knocked on the door. "Hey, Kat?"

"Yeah Dem? I'll be out shortly."

"That's okay. Just want to let you know Sam's here."

"Oh. Tell her to wait in my room."

"Okay." Dem closed the door.

Oh Lord, sooner than later. Kat started to hurry as she washed her hair and her body. Should she shave? Maybe she should. Sam could wait. *What the hell?* Kat just wanted to go to bed. This could have waited till morning. She got out of the shower and dried off. She wrapped her hair in a towel and put on her bathrobe and brushed her teeth. She was trying to stall the encounter, not looking forward to the impending confrontation.

She walked out of the bathroom and into her bedroom. "Sam! What are you doing here, it's so late."

Sam sat on Kat's bed, looking through a magazine. "I just needed to see you is all. I thought you were staying at your mom's tonight."

"If you thought that, then why are you here?" Kat retorted slyly.

"Kat, I need to know what's going on with you. Where were you tonight? My friend Angie called and told me that she saw you and some guy down at The Tavern. Why are you lying to me?" she asked aggressively.

Kat blinked, irritated. "Why are you spying on me, Sam? This is so unnecessary. I can't do anything without you checking up on me. I don't like it."

"Well, it's obvious that you're not being honest with me."

Kat walked around her bedroom, busying herself with putting away her newly washed laundry. She thought about being honest with Sam, but she knew that her words would hurt her. She also knew that Sam didn't take well to rejection. She hated to have to explain herself.

She turned to face Sam, opened her mouth, and was surprised at the words that came out. "I'm not being honest? Honest about what, Sam? I went and had drinks with an old friend of mine. We grew up together. He lived down the street from me. I was planning on going home—that was my plan this afternoon—but then he called me tonight and asked me if I wanted to catch up. So we did. What the hell does it matter to you?"

"You've been acting weird lately, Kat. I sense it. I sense you don't want to be around me. I'm scared." Sam sat on the bed and started to cry.

Kat thought about Charles. She wanted to tell Sam that she was curious, curious about men. She wanted to explain to her that it wasn't entirely her fault; it was just how she felt.

"Sam, this isn't going to work between us. I think you know this. We are not the same people. You seem to always want to change me, like I'm not good enough. The truth is I like my life and I don't want to change. I don't think you will ever accept me," Kat lectured. Kat thought about all the secrets she kept from Sam. How could a relationship work if she felt the need to keep so many secrets?

"You're good enough for me, Kat," Sam said, sitting up straight on the bed. "I love you. I don't want you to change." Sam moved from the bed and stood in front of her. She looked at Kat, her eyes full of tears, pleading with her. "Please Kat, we can work on this. We can work it out."

Kat sighed. "Sam, you know in your heart you deserve better and I deserve to be with someone who accepts me for who I am." She needed to be with a man, she knew; she needed to see what it was like; she needed to know for herself.

"No Kat, you are the only one who could make me happy." Sam stepped closer to her. She reached out to embrace her. "I only need you, Kat," she whispered.

Kat sighed, a heavy sigh. This wasn't going to be easy.

"Kiss me, Kat. Please, I need you," she begged. Kat looked at Sam. Sam started to kiss her face, her cheeks and her lips. "You smell so good, Kat," she said softly. She kissed her neck; she took her hair down and out of the towel.

"Sam, this really isn't a good idea," Kat said weakly.

"Don't talk. Just let me touch you. Just stand here and let me feel you."

Kat stood still. She didn't respond to her physically. She just let her do her thing. Sam had always been very good at lovemaking. She was very selfless.

"This is the last time, Sam. We need a break from each other. Do you understand?" Kat said forcefully.

"Shhh…let's just enjoy each other tonight, Kat. We'll talk about this again tomorrow." Sam untied her bathrobe and put her hands around Kat's waist. Her breathing was heavy as she ran her fingers around Kat's body, up her stomach and down her back. She kissed her passionately, pulling her tightly toward her body.

She caressed her breasts; she bent down, slowly sucking on her nipples, biting her gently. She removed her bathrobe, dropping it to the floor. "Spread your legs for me, Kat."

Kat hated when Sam was bossy in her normal day-to-day life, but when she told her what to do during sex, it completely turned her on. She spread her legs for her, feeling completely vulnerable. Sam knelt down in front of her. "Spread them more, Kat," she said. Kat did what she told her. Sam kissed her belly as her hands massaged her ass. She moved them around her bottom and then massaged her inner thighs. Kat moaned lightly and closed her eyes. She thought, *Could it be this good with a man? Is this what it's like? Stop thinking! Just enjoy.*

Sam kissed her along her inner thighs until she reached her most sensitive area. She slowly poked her tongue at her, separating her lips and sucking on them. She sucked on her sweet spot while she took her fingers and gently put them in her vagina. Kat moaned more deeply. Sam was making her dizzy, she felt so good. Sam continued to tease her, touching her perfectly and driving her crazy.

Kat pulled her up. She kissed Sam's face. She really was beautiful, so sexy. Kat began to undress her. She removed her shirt and then her pants. Sam was wearing a soft, pink, lacy top and matching satin underwear. Her breasts were full and practically falling out of her bra. Kat kissed the tops of them. She kissed her nipples through the thin, light material. She began to kiss her stomach, all the way down past her waist. She caressed her and brought her mouth down hard on top of her underwear. She smelled so good and sweet. "Please Kat, take them off," Sam begged.

"No Sam, be still and relax," Kat said smoothly.

"Please, touch me," she whimpered. Kat took her fingers and slid them inside her panties.

"You're so wet. Am I turning you on?" Kat asked roughly.

Sam moaned loudly. "I don't know if I can take it any longer."

"Lay on the bed, Sam, and I'll finish undressing you."

Sam walked back toward the bed and lay down on the covers. "You look so sexy," Kat said as she crawled on top of her and kissed her mouth. She removed her bra and kissed her naked breasts. She sucked on them hard, causing Sam to gasp a little in pain. Kat removed Sam's panties and pressed open her legs. Kat stopped and slowly placed her fingers inside Sam's body, causing Sam to yell out in desire.

"Oh god!" she screamed.

Kat put her tongue on Sam's clitoris and sucked at her, moving her fingers slowly, in and out. Sam moaned and moved slightly on the bed. Sam sat up to face Kat, their breasts touching each other as they continued to caress each other's bodies. Sam kissed her neck and pulled Kat toward her, touching Kat delicately with her fingers, teasing her in the same manner, driving her wild.

"Oh god, Sam," she yelled. "I'm going to cum."

"Me too, Kat...."

Their bodies shuddered and convulsed, Sam rubbing harder and harder on Kat and Kat on her. They both screamed while they orgasmed, their bodies vibrating inside and out. They collapsed on the bed together. They lay in silence as they tried to catch their breath.

That was a big mistake.

Sam turned to Kat, kissed her face and cupped her breast with her hand. "How could you even consider leaving me when we have such wonderful sex like that?" she asked, exhausted.

Kat laughed at her. "Sex isn't our problem, Sam."

Sam frowned at her. She sat back up and put her bra on, then her panties. "I love you, Kat. I'll never let you go," she stated firmly as she dressed.

Kat looked at Sam as she lay back down next to her, Kat's hand on Sam's pillow. "I know, Sam. I know."

CHAPTER 23

Jack

Work on the farm was hard but school was going better than I expected. Everyone was so friendly and welcoming. My schedule was busy and sometimes I felt too tired to care one way or the other. I woke up early in the morning with Pop to feed the cattle and tend to the horses. I washed up, ate a quick breakfast, and then was off to school. When I got home, it was more of the same. Work with Pop, tend to the corn or the orchard, eat dinner, do homework, and then bed. My grandfather said it's good for me. "Hard work is rewarding," he lectured. I guess I'm just not used to it. Susie Mae says I'm tired because I'm growing.

"You're growing, boy! I can't keep a lick of food around here, thanks to you!" she laughed as she teased me. "I need another chef to help me feed everybody."

"You're an excellent chef, Susie Mae. You're the best around town," I told her. This always made her smile and stopped her complaining. Flattery, I learned, gets you a lot of things, like an extra piece of apple pie. I guess I am growing. I'm definitely stronger than I've ever been.

The football coach at school keeps after me to join the team. "Jack, have you ever played football under the lights in a real stadium?"

I always answer, "No coach, can't say that I have."

"Well, I should think you might want to consider it, give it a try." I always shook my head no. My grandfather needed me now. He was relying on me. I thought about it though, joining the team. Back in Connecticut the boys and I played plenty of touch football. Some of my greatest memories of my brother and my friends were of the times we would play baseball or football. I miss having friends. I miss my brother.

My friend Adam was interested in science and paranormal activities, rather than sports. I swear he was obsessed with UFOs and ghost hunts. On occasion, I'd let him drag me to one of the town meetings regarding the unidentified findings of late. The endless conversation about strange markings in the cornfields and the sightings of this object and that are all very interesting, but it felt like I was in a science fiction movie. Adam was kind in including me in everything he did. I oftentimes said no and blamed my inability to come with him on the fact that I needed to help my grandfather. This only satisfied him for a while and then he got tired of my excuses and forced me to join him. I figured I owed him. He did take me under his wing this senior year at school. It'd been easy going ever since.

I appreciated the ease of life there. My life back home wasn't so easy. I felt on edge, never knowing what may happen next. When I wake up here, at our farm, I know what I need to do. I know exactly how my day will go and what is expected of me. It feels good to be needed. I have responsibility now. I try to ignore the loneliness. As much as I try to fit in here, a part of me is missing. I'm not sure how to fix that. Pop tells me it will take time. He tells me I'm still mourning my mother. I don't feel like I'm mourning my mother. My mother has been gone for several years now. I feel like I'm mourning the life I used to have and the life I wish still existed. I'm mourning the loss of my brother, the loss of a mother that I never had. My life with Pop is great, but I'm still missing something. Something's got to change.

CHAPTER 24

Lucy

I came home the night of the dance with a renewed determination to find Jack. My father was waiting for me. He seemed irritated. "You're mother was waiting all night for you," he yelled. I stood there, shocked by his assault.

"It's only 12:00! What time was I supposed to be home? Thomas came for us. I didn't know I was late!"

My dad looked tired. "I'm sorry, honey. You're not late. You're mother was just worried and you know how she gets, she gets confused."

"I'm sorry, Dad, I'm home now. Do you want me to go tell her?" I asked.

"No, I think she finally went to sleep. Let her rest for now."

"Okay."

"How was the prom? You look lovely, by the way. I'm sorry I missed you before you left."

"The dance was fun, no big deal. Don't worry about it, Mom took about a hundred pictures."

"Well, I'm glad you had fun. I'm going up now, going to bed." My dad bent down to kiss me. "Goodnight Lucy."

"Night, Dad."

I walked up the stairs shortly after and headed to Kathryn's room. She wasn't home. Figures. I'll never get a hold of her. I wondered where Thomas was off to tonight. He couldn't wait to drop me off. Thomas doesn't have a curfew. He's probably going to a party with some friends. Kathryn stays out all night too. Seems like everyone around here doesn't have a curfew except for me. What's the big deal? I poked my head into Kaylan and Jessica's bedroom. They were sound asleep. They looked so cute. I wanted to take my dress off and wash my face. I quietly went into my bedroom and started to undress.

I looked up at myself in the mirror. I jumped briefly as my mother startled me with her sudden appearance in my doorway. "God, Mom, you scared me half to death!" I turned around to look at her. She stared at me. She didn't smile. She didn't say anything, just turned around and walked away. I stared at the empty doorway, baffled. Maybe she's sleepwalking. I shook it off and put on my pajamas. I climbed into my bed and thought about Jack.

How could I find out where he's staying? How could I find information? Charles must know something. Tomorrow I will hunt for Kathryn. I need her help now. My heart jumped with excitement at the thought of finding Jack again. Seeing him, hearing his voice. It's something I needed to do. The small voice in my head wouldn't let me forget him. My heart could never forget.

CHAPTER 25

Amelia

Amelia called Lucy the next day. "Danny has been talking about you to everyone," she said excitedly.

"What? How do you know this already? It's 10:00 in the morning, how do you already have gossip?" Lucy asked.

Amelia laughed. "I know everything and I know for sure that he likes you."

"Well, that's nice, but I'm not at all interested. I think he's painfully shy."

"Well, you wouldn't think so if you heard some of the things he's been saying. Things like, 'Lucy's the prettiest girl in school and she so kind to everyone. I would really like to spend more time with her.' Things like that."

"Tell him I have a boyfriend."

"But you don't."

"Well, I will someday and it's not going to be Danny. Just forget it, Amelia."

"You're so difficult!" she complained.

Lucy laughed. "I am not. Tell me about your night anyway. How was Izzy's?"

"It was fine. No big news to report." Amelia sat back on her couch and grinned slyly. When Thomas had whispered in her ear after she got out of his car, he asked if she could get out of Izzy's sleepover planned for later that night. She smiled as she thought about the night before. She thought about Thomas and how he picked her up from Izzy's. She thought about how he took her to a local motel and how he had decorated the room with candles and how he played soft music. She thought about how they made love and talked and kissed and held each other all night. What a magical night she had. "It was actually very boring, Lucy," she lied. "You didn't miss a thing."

"I have some things to do today, but I'll call you tonight, when I get home," Lucy said. "I would love to sit and talk with you. I have some things to tell you."

"I have something to tell you too, Lucy. We'll talk later then?"

"Yes, I'll call you later."

"All right, bye then."

"Bye, Amelia."

Amelia thought about what she and Thomas had talked about. They'd decided to tell Lucy they were an item. Thomas didn't want to waste one more day trying to hide it any longer. "I'll be going back to college in the fall, Amelia," he'd told her. "I don't want to waste any more of our time together. If Lucy can't accept it, then so be it." Amelia knew that he was right. She was nervous about Lucy's reaction. She wondered, too, what it was Lucy needed to talk to her about. Maybe she knew or suspected them. Oh well, it'd have to wait until tonight. Amelia leaned back and enjoyed her memories from last night. What a great night. Amelia smiled.

CHAPTER 26

Lucy

My mother walked slowly down the stairs, groggy from her sleep. "Hi, Mom!" I said brightly to awaken her senses.

"Good morning, Lucy. How was the dance, sweetheart?"

"It was good. Do you want a cup of coffee?" My mother needed her morning coffee before anyone should try to talk to her. I poured her a cup and hoped that she was up for a conversation.

"Sorry that you waited for me to come home last night. Dad said you were upset that I was late?"

"What is he talking about? I wasn't upset, honey."

"Do you remember coming to my room last night? You were acting weird and staring at me."

My mother laughed. "Don't be silly."

"Do you remember?" I asked.

"Of course I do. I was really sleepy last night. I took a sleeping pill. Perhaps I was just a little drowsy, that's all," she explained. "Sorry if I was *creepy*," she added in her weird voice.

"Stop it, Mom. You're worrying me. Something seems off with you. You're forgetting things."

My mother put down her coffee and came and wrapped her arms around me. "I don't want you to worry about me, Lucy. I'm fine."

"If you need my help, Mom, just tell me. I'll try to help you any way that I can," I said.

"You've always been my favorite. You do know this, right?" my mother asked as she winked at me. "I truly appreciate your concern and I promise you, if I need your help, I will ask for it. Okay, honey?"

"Okay, Mom. I love you."

"I love you too, sweetheart."

I lingered around the kitchen for a moment, deciding if I should ask about Kathryn. "Mom, do you have any idea where Kathryn is?" I asked. My mother looked at me, disgusted with my question.

"Kat probably stayed at Demetry's house last night. That's where she stays when she's not here. Although she doesn't know that I know this." My mother stood from her seat and angrily opened one of the kitchen cabinets to grab more sugar for her coffee. She slammed the cabinet shut as she continued talking, her words becoming agitated, spit escaping her mouth as she spoke. "I don't know what kind of fool she thinks I am or why on earth she thinks I would just let her disappear without knowing where she goes all the time." My mother began riffling through her pocketbook, her face determined and focused on finding nothing. "Her only saving grace is that I think Demetry is a safe and healthy choice for a companion. I'm hoping the more time they spend together, the more likely they may fall in love and get married. I can only hope for these things because I don't think your sister will ever be motivated enough to find a decent boyfriend."

"Mom, don't be so hard on Kathryn. She's just easygoing. She'll never be in a rush or have any kind of sense of urgency. It's not in her nature."

My mother sighed. "I'm already getting a headache and it's only 8:00 in the morning. I have a long day ahead of me."

"Do you have Demetry's phone number?"

"No, but he lives off Bartlett Lane, in a small yellow house. His mother and I talk regularly. They think we're fools."

"I'm sure they don't think that, Mom. They just like their privacy. I need to talk to her." I took a step toward the door. "I'm going to take a walk over there. Is there anything you need while I'm out? Do you want me to do anything before I leave?"

Mom looked at me. "No, but you can give that daughter of mine a message. Tell her that it would be nice to see her occasionally. She *does* still live here."

"Yeah, okay Mom, I'll tell her."

I couldn't wait to leave the house. My mother's moods were so unpredictable, and she was getting irritable. I didn't want to think about that now. I was hopeful Kathryn could help me find Charles.

I walked the few blocks until I reached Bartlett Lane. It was a beautiful summer morning. The birds were chirping and the flowers were in bloom. All the trees had their buds on them. The air smelled sweet like fresh-cut grass and the neighborhoods were busy with activity. People were out doing chores in their yards and waving and talking to each other. It was a nice walk.

When I finally reached the small yellow house, I noticed how cute and quaint the gardens were around the front yard. *Demetry must have a green thumb*, I thought to myself. I strolled up the walkway and knocked on the front door. I waited. Finally, Kat opened the door.

"Lucy! What are you doing here?" she asked, surprised.

"I need to talk to you, Kathryn. Is it okay if I come in?"

"Of course, come in."

"The gardens are so pretty up the walkway. Demetry must be good at gardening," I said.

Kat laughed. "No, I have the green thumb around here. Although he does as well, but in other ways."

I looked at her, not understanding.

She laughed again. "Never mind. How did you find me?"

"Mom told me where you were."

"*Mom?*" Kat sat down in a chair. "How does Mom know where I am?"

"She says you're not as slick as you think you are. Also, she wants you to come home and visit her."

Kat stared at me while she tried to digest what I was trying to tell her. Demetry walked into the kitchen.

173

"Hey Dem," Kat said. "This is my younger sister Lucy."

"Hey Lucy. I remember you when you were a little pipsqueak," Dem said, smiling.

I nodded hello to him. "Nice to meet you," I said.

"Lucy, do you want a cup of coffee?" Kat stood to fill the pot and turn the coffee maker on.

"Sure, that sounds really good."

"Have a seat here, Lucy." Dem cleared a spot at the table for me.

"I'm so surprised you're here. Why do you need to see me?" Kat asked. I looked at Kathryn. She looked relaxed and very comfortable in her environment.

"Are you two dating?" I asked. Demetry started to laugh out loud as Kathryn turned and punched him in his arm.

"Are you crazy?" Kathryn asked me.

"Sorry, I just don't get it. It's like you live here with him."

"I know, it probably does appear to be strange, but we're just friends. Demetry is my best friend in the whole world. Aren't you, Dem?"

174

"Sure am." Dem sat in his chair reading a newspaper. He nodded his head and barely looked up at the two of us. Kathryn leaned over and kissed him on his cheek. I watched the two of them. Demetry looked up at her and smiled. He was obviously very fond of her.

"Anyway, I came here to ask you something. Do you remember when we went for that walk in the woods that day? We had a talk about Jack and other things." I looked at her, hoping she remembered without me getting into more detail about what *else* we did that day. Kathryn was laughing again.

"I remember. Hey Dem, remember I told you about taking my sister for a walk and how we shared a joint?"

"Oh yeah! That was you little pipsqueak?"

"Yes, it was I." I smiled, embarrassed. "*Anyway*," I said, pressing on, "do you remember Charles? Charles Nimchak. Jack's brother?"

Kathryn's eyes jumped up as she looked at me.

Demetry's eyes also looked up at me, finally interested in what I was about to say.

"Yeah, what about him?" she asked cautiously.

"I really need to find him. It's important. Thomas went out with him a few months back and I asked him about Jack.

175

He wouldn't tell me anything, but I have the feeling that he knows something. I really need to see him again."

Kathryn sat with her coffee in her chair. "You want to see if Charles knows how to find Jack? Is that right?"

"Yes, exactly right," I said firmly.

"I don't think he knows where he is, Lucy."

"He must have some idea."

"I don't know," Kathryn said, shaking her head. "I can tell you one thing, though. I do know how to find Charles."

I jumped up off my chair. "You *do*?!"

"Yes, I do."

Dem chimed in, "She went on a date with him the other night."

Kathryn kicked Demetry's chair. "Shut up, Dem!"

"*You did?!*" I said, shocked. I couldn't believe it. "This is fantastic! Can you call him, can we go see him?" I asked. I was practically jumping up and down.

"Okay! Okay!" Kathryn said, holding her hands up and motioning for me to calm down. "Let me make a phone call. I'll see what I can do. Please, sit down, relax and finish your coffee. I'm going to clean up, take a shower, and get dressed.

Dem, entertain my sister for me, please." Kathryn walked out of the kitchen in a hurry.

Dem looked up at me. "Have you any interest in potted plants, Lucy?"

Kathryn screamed from her room, "*Demetry!*"

Demetry stood and put his arm around me and started to guide me through the small house. "I'm just kidding. Let me take you around to the gardens we have out back. I'll show you a little something about your sister that may surprise you."

I looked up at Dem and smiled. I thought to myself, *I like this guy.*

CHAPTER 27

Jack

Weekends were always busy on the farm. We got plenty of visitors who wanted to poke around and buy some of our fresh produce and vegetables. Susie Mae ran our little storefront where customers parked their cars and walked around the main barn and looked at the cows with their children. When the orchards were ripe for picking, they could also pick their own apples and pumpkins.

Pop said the income was crucial to the farm. It kept the money flow going and the animals fed for the year. After the crowds left, I went around and picked up any garbage that was left behind. I made sure the barns were in good order and that the animals were settled in for the night.

Alex, one of Pop's workers, walked into the cow barn. "Hey Jack! Your pop wants you back up at the house. He's waiting for you."

"I'll be up in a few minutes," I replied.

"Go ahead, go up. I'll finish these chores for you," he offered.

I looked at Alex and smiled. "Good! I'm glad I left cleaning the cow dung for last!" I said as I slowly jogged for the door.

"Get out of here, you little punk." Alex grabbed the pitchfork from my hand.

I laughed, "Thanks, Alex! I'll see you later."

"I'll need your help tomorrow, boy. You come find me after school," he hollered after me as I waved at him.

"Will do!"

I walked up the long stone driveway from the barn to the main house. The farmhouse was white with a large wraparound porch. Susie Mae had her flowers in the planter boxes, the benches and the porch swings in beautiful order. She also had her special rocking chairs, one for her and one for Pop. I thought about Pop and Susie Mae. This farm would be nothing without her. She made life cozy. Without her, the men would ruin this place. Susie kept the house clean, food in the kitchen and she took good care of all of us. She took good care of Pop. He would be lost without her. I believed they loved each other in that way, although Susie had her own sleeping quarters on the farm. She stayed in the small guesthouse behind the main house. I've never been inside. She wouldn't allow it, but I wondered. I wondered about her and Pop. I smiled as I thought about the two of them. They were very cute together.

As I approached the porch I could hear voices coming from within the kitchen. I could also smell dinner—it smelled like Susie was making a pot roast—and I was starving. I opened the kitchen door and stopped. It was Coach Franco. Coach stood and walked toward me and shook my hand. "Hey Jack," he said kindly.

I smiled. "Hello, sir."

Susie Mae, at the kitchen sink, looked at me and winked. Pop stood from the table and asked me to sit down for a minute. My heart was beating faster than normal. I knew why Coach was here. I wasn't sure if I was nervous or excited or if I would be disappointed.

Pop started, "Coach Franco has been telling us what a great football player he thinks you would be. He says he's been asking you to join the team."

Coach Franco added, "You're a strong, young man, Jack. I know your grandparents are very proud of you."

"We're extremely proud of our boy," Susie added to confirm the coach's view.

All three adults stared at me, waiting for me to speak. I wasn't sure what to say.

"Why haven't you mentioned this to me?" Pop asked.

I looked at my grandfather. His eyes were full of pride and respect. "Pop, I want to be here with you, on the farm. Football will take all of my time. How can I do it all? I can't help you and do my studies and play ball. It's impossible."

My grandfather started to laugh. He placed his hands on my shoulders. "Do you think we will fall apart if you are unable to help us every day after school? We've run this farm for decades without you, Jack. I do know a thing or two."

I put my head down, embarrassed. "I know that, Pop, but I don't want to disappoint you. My first priority is to you and Susie Mae. It just feels wrong to play football. It feels selfish."

Coach started to stand. "I think I'll leave you all to talk about these matters privately."

Pop and I stood and said our goodbyes. Coach stopped and shook my hand. "I hope to see you at practice tomorrow, Jack. We have a big season ahead of us. You would make a great addition to the team."

"Thank you, Coach. Thanks for stopping by," I said as he walked to the door.

"Goodbye, folks." Coach dipped his hat and head, paying respect to Susie Mae and Pop. I stood there watching him, and then I turned around and looked at Pop and Susie.

Pop had a serious look on his face. "You're playing! No arguments about it."

"Don't argue with your grandfather, Jack. Don't waste your time," Susie added.

"Decisions made," Pop said as he came over to embrace me. He looked into my eyes. "I want you to know something. My life changed when you came here. My life is better now. I couldn't love you more than if you were my own son. I only want the best for you. I want you to experience everything life has to offer. This farm will be yours one day, Jack. You have a whole life of chores ahead of you. You need to understand that. Do you understand?"

I looked up at Pop and nodded. I tried to fight back the tears of appreciation that I felt for him. "So, what do you say, Susie? Are you ready for some football?!"

Susie smiled at my pop. "I can't wait. I love to watch football!"

I stared at both of them. I hugged my grandfather. "Thank you, Pop."

"You're welcome, son. Let's sit down and eat. I'm starving."

I smiled. "Sounds good to me."

My heart was pounding; I felt so excited. I couldn't wait to be on the team, to be a part of something again.

CHAPTER 28

Mama

Lucy left in a hurry as Mama watched her scamper down the street, hoping that she would be able to find Kathryn and get whatever information she needed from her. Mama also needed to find Joseph and apologize to him for her behavior. She knew he was probably in the garage, tinkering on some small project that he'd been working on. She still needed to talk to him about last night. She didn't know what the big deal was. If she wanted to wait for her child, she could wait, however long that may be. It may seem crazy to him, but she wanted to do what was necessary and what felt comfortable to her.

"Jessica?" she started, catching her daughter's attention. "I need to go out into the garage and talk to your father; can you keep an eye on Mikey? Don't tease him. Just keep him out of trouble."

Mama grabbed a light jacket; she was sure that it was chilly in the garage. She opened the door and walked out into the fresh morning air. It was bright and sunny out. It looked like a beautiful day. She didn't know why she felt so drained. She constantly felt dread, like something bad could happen at any moment. She was always worried. She didn't know how to shake it. She often felt confused. This was true. Joseph had no idea how much or how often she felt this way. She was thankful for the times when all the children were out of the house or at school and Joseph was at work. Sometimes she would sit and stare and think for hours, waiting for the children to come home. When they did come home, she would snap out of it and return to her normal caretaking activities. She just couldn't figure out why this was happening to her. She used to feel normal. She didn't feel normal anymore. She couldn't always control her thoughts. It was so overwhelming. She was afraid to tell Joseph the truth, but it was getting harder to hide it. Her outbursts were uncontrollable.

She opened the garage door to see if Joseph was inside, working. The garage was cluttered and packed full with children's toys, lawnmowers, furniture, and everything else under the sun. Joseph had a little woodworking area toward the back of the garage where he could work on his projects. He was great at fixing old antiques and making them look new again. Her house was full of old pieces of furniture that they'd acquired from tag sales. She loved his handiness.

"Joseph? Can we talk?"

Joseph looked up from his bench. "Sure, honey. How are you, are you okay?" He was kind when he spoke to her, even though she was so rotten to him the night before.

"I just wanted to apologize for last night. I don't know what has gotten hold of me. I am truly sorry for the things that I said. I know you were just trying to help me." Her voice cracked. She knew her eyes were watering but she continued to try to hold back her tears.

Joseph stood and looked at her, then took a few steps toward her, held out his hand, and pulled her into a strong embrace. Joseph was a rock. Mama didn't know what she would do without him. He was everything to her. He worked so hard to support their family. She held him tightly; she didn't want to let go. He stood back from her and looked into her face.

"I love you, Sarah. I'm really concerned about you. I think it's time we go see a doctor. Maybe someone can help us."

She shook her head no. "I can control this, Joseph, and I'm okay. I'll figure it out, I promise you. I'll start to exercise more, I'll try to get more rest, and I'll learn to be more patient with the children. This will help control the anxiety, you'll see." She started to cry. "I'm sorry, Joseph."

"It's alright, sweetheart. Stop crying." Joseph looked at his wife and wiped the tears that had fallen on her cheeks. "I'm sorry too, darling. I know I should be more helpful to you. I will try harder to take some of the load off your plate. Okay, honey?" Joseph kissed her softly on her lips and they embraced each other.

She wished she didn't have to go back inside. She had anxiety when she went inside the house, with the kids. She knew she shouldn't feel this way, but it was true. She should probably go back.

"I'm going to check on the kids." She had to force the words from her tongue.

"Okay, dear. I'll be in shortly."

Mama walked back out of the garage and grudgingly up the porch steps to the house.

Dread. All she felt was dread.

CHAPTER 29

Lucy

Kathryn and I walked up five flights of stairs to get to Charles' apartment. I could tell Kathryn was feeling a little uncomfortable. She seemed nervous. I was feeling a little anxiety too. The neighborhood that Charles lived in was run down. There was garbage thrown around in the hallway, a broken light fixture, and graffiti on the walls. You could hear one of the neighbors yelling at a child. Kathryn grabbed my hand. "I hope Charles doesn't get upset that we came here," she said, concerned. "I tried to call him several times, but he didn't answer."

As we walked up the stairs, I thought about the home Charles and Jack used to live in. Rundown in its own way, full of rotten memories. "I'm sure he'll be surprised to see us," I said as cheerfully convincing as I could. "Do you know which apartment is his?"

"Not really. The mailbox said 5-2, so I assume that it's fifth floor, apartment two." Kat shrugged. When we reached the fifth floor, there where four doors in the hallway. None of which had numbers on them.

"Now what?" I asked.

"Let's knock on the second door to the right. Keep your fingers crossed."

"You knock!" I said as I pushed her toward the door. She started to laugh nervously.

"Stop it, Lucy. I'm frightened. Someone might steal us!" she whispered with a giggle.

"They might steal you, but I'll be running fast down the flight of stairs we just came up from!" I replied.

"You'd leave me?" she asked sadly.

"You better run, Kat, if anything funny goes down!" I warned.

"That's our plan then? To run?"

"Yup," I said. "Now knock."

Before we could knock, the door opened wide and an elderly man was standing there, holding a cup of coffee, dressed in only his underwear.

"Oh god," I said.

"Um, excuse me sir. We don't mean to bother you but we were looking for our friend, Charles," Kat said nervously.

Just then Charles opened the door behind us, across the hallway.

"What the hell are you two doing here?" he demanded.

Kathryn sighed with relief. "*Oh*, Charles. There you are."

The old man tried to talk but Charles yelled at him. "Get back in your apartment and put some clothes on. Damn fool, you leave these girls alone!"

"Fuck you!" the old man said grumpily as he slammed the door shut.

"Get in here," Charles said, scanning the hallway.

Kathryn and I walked in. Surprisingly, it was very clean and neat on the inside.

"What are you doing here, Kathryn?" Charles said with a bright smile on his face. If he was annoyed with us, he didn't show it. "Hi Lucy," he said to me.

"Hi Charles, I hope we're not interrupting you."

"No, I was just getting ready for work. I'm on second shift today."

"Oh, well we won't keep you long," Kathryn said. "Lucy really needed to speak to you about Jack."

Charles' eyes met mine with a shared understanding. "Jack?" he said. "I told you, Lucy, I don't know where Jack is. I've been looking for him myself."

I stood and approached Charles. "There must be something we can do; there's got to be a way," I said.

Charles paced the living room floor in a small circle, shaking his head. "I've looked in all the right places. I've gone to the police. They had nothing. I've gone to social services, nothing. It's like he just disappeared, like that night never happened." Charles finally slumped in a chair.

"What exactly happened, Charles?" I asked. "Can you tell me what happened that night, with the police?"

Charles looked distressed. Kathryn went and sat in a chair next to him. He looked up at her and said, "I'm glad you're here, Kat. I really enjoyed our time together the other night."

Kathryn smiled and nodded in agreement with him. "I'm sorry that we're pressing you, Charles. If you don't want to talk about it, we'll understand."

"No, it's okay," Charles replied, looking at me. "I don't understand," he went on. "Why are you so concerned with Jack? What happened between you and my brother that day? Can you tell me anything about that day yourself?"

I looked up at Charles and my sister. "Yes, I can. Jack asked me to come say goodbye to him before I left for my grandmother's up in Vermont. I brought him a plate of cookies. When I got to your house, Jack and I talked. He was very upset; he said you went to go look for your mother. I stayed with Jack for hours that day and we cleaned the house together. After I left, I saw you in the police car, and that was the last I heard from either one of you. I felt so awful." I went on. "For years I've thought about Jack and that day. I've worried about him ever since." I put my head in my hands.

Charles chuckled a little. "I went back to my house the night I ran away from the foster home they placed me in. I walked around the house in shock at how clean everything was. I thought it was strange that my brother had done such a nice job cleaning. Now I understand."

I looked up and gave a half smile to Charles.

"The police picked me up that afternoon at the scrapyard down by Broad Street," Charles began. "I know a man down there who knows everything. I thought I would go there and ask him about my mother. See if he'd heard anything around town. Apparently the police had wanted to interrogate him as well. When the police arrived, they started to ask me questions. I told them I was looking for my mother and I gave them a description of what she looked like. The police officer asked me if I had any relatives that could help them identify a body. I told them that we had no relatives in Connecticut and that I was my mother's oldest son. The police officer asked if I felt grown up enough to come with them to identify some belongings. They found a woman deceased the night before who might have been my mother."

Kathryn and I sat there listening to Charles, both our hearts breaking as he told us his story. He was just a kid back then, a boy, just barely sixteen. Kathryn put her hand on Charles' leg. He looked up at her and she encouraged him to continue.

"That could have been the worst day of my life. I had to identify my mother and then I had to break it to my brother that she was dead. When the police brought me home that night, we picked up Jack and brought him to the police station. We were both placed in foster care for the night. I had been so upset and distraught. I wasn't thinking clearly. I ran away. A few days later, after the shock of everything had worn off, I realized what I had done. I had abandoned Jack." He paused and breathed deeply. "I never forgave myself. I thought maybe he would return here when he was old enough and that's why I came back. I figured I could wait a couple years to see if he returns. Maybe he's looking for me as well."

I agreed with Charles. "That's seems perfectly possible," I said.

Kathryn turned to Charles to embrace him. "You were just a kid, Charles; you can't beat yourself up about this. You experienced a very traumatic situation."

Charles shook his head. "I know, Kat, but it's hard to forget. I missed him so much. He was my best friend. I should have been there to take care of him."

"Can you remember anything about the foster people Jack was staying with?" I pressed. "Anything at all?"

"I know Jack mentioned my grandfather. He thought we could go live with him," Charles said.

"You have a grandfather!?" I asked.

"Yes. He lives out west, but I don't know his name or what state he's in or anything." Charles looked at me, his voice full of frustration.

"Well, that's good information. There has to be a way to find his name. What about your mother's death certificate? They always list family names on birth certificates and death certificates. Do you remember where she was born?" I asked.

"No, I don't, but she died here, so maybe the town hall?" he suggested.

I jumped up. "Yes! That might be something."

Charles stood and looked at his clock. "I have to go to work still. I wish I could stay and help you two." Charles grabbed my arm. "Do you think we can find him, Lucy? I would really like to try."

I smiled at Charles. "I'm not giving up. Are you?"

He smiled in return, a hint of hope spreading across his features. "No, Lucy. I *need* to find my brother."

"Great, then Kat and I will go to the town hall. We'll do everything we can to find some information. Do you want to meet later? Back at Kat's?"

Charles looked at Kat. "Would that be okay, Kat? I'll stop by after work, around 8:00."

Kathryn looked at Charles. "We'll be there. I'll save you dinner too," she said happily.

Charles smiled. "Let's get out of here then. I need to go."

Charles, Kat, and I walked down the stairs and out of the building, a renewed sense of energy and purpose in all of us.

CHAPTER 30

Jack

I ran down the hallway of my childhood home. I tried to scream but nothing would come out. I looked around me; I felt Lucy was with me but I couldn't see her. I could feel my body move but I couldn't wake up. I could hear the gargling noises that I was making but still, I was unable to shake the nightmare. There was someone chasing me. He was grabbing at my arm. I was trying to run and watch the man behind me and look for Lucy. I see her. I could see her eyes. She's hiding. Good, she's safe. The man, he's almost got me. I tried to yell to Lucy. "Don't move, Lucy!" but I struggled with the words. She's coming out of hiding. "NO, LUCY!" I tried to yell again, but nothing would come out. He was going to see her. He was going to kill her.

"NOOOOO!"

I bolted up in a sitting position from my sleep. My heart was pounding and sweat beaded around my back and neck. I sat on the edge of my bed, my hands on my face, trying to slow my heartbeat. I collapsed back onto my pillow. I closed my eyes and tried to calm my nerves. It's like my subconscious wouldn't let me forget. Susie Mae tells me my brain is trying to heal itself, but I don't know if that's true.

I'm miserable the next day. Football training was so intense. There were only a few weeks before the first big game. Talent scouts were at the school almost every weekend. They came and looked at you. Assessed your skills and talent for college recruitment. I wasn't very concerned about this since I didn't intend to play college ball. Coach seemed to care, but he didn't know my history. He didn't know where my heart was, with Pop and the farm.

Coach was very pleased I could replace the senior quarterback, who had suffered from an arm injury the season before. Apparently, I had great aim and accuracy. Pop couldn't be happier. I would see him some afternoons at the field. He would show up to watch us scrimmage. It was great to see the excitement in his eyes when we talked. He truly enjoyed this.

One thing I could say about football is that my social life definitely benefited from being the new star quarterback. I had no idea what a barn party was until I joined the team.

Every weekend someone was having a party or a bonfire. I was stuck in my lonely little world, who knew? Pop had been great too. He encouraged me every time, go and have fun.

"Meet a nice girl," he would say. I smiled and waved him off.

"I don't have time for girls, Pop."

Pop shook his head. "You make time, then."

I didn't want him to worry so I would say, "I will, Pop." I didn't think about girls. The only one I thought about was Lucy. I read her note every day; I held it in my hand. Lucy was beautiful and sweet and she had compassion for people. I could never let go of Lucy. She's the one. She's the only connection I had left to my home back east. I'll go back someday. I hope. Maybe. I don't know. I will.

CHAPTER 31

Lucy

Kathryn and I stood at the corner of Main Street and waited for the town bus to come by. I turned to Kathryn. "We could probably walk, Kat. It's only about six blocks from here."

"We're not walking, Lucy," Kathryn hissed. "Have you taken a good look around us? This is not the neighborhood I want to go walking around and exploring in, looking lost like we don't know where we are going."

"Okay, Kat. " I looked at her with wide eyes full of fear. I laughed as I teased her.

We didn't have to wait long; the bus came right on schedule. We asked the bus driver to drop us off downtown near the police station and town hall, and he did. We climbed down the stairs of the bus and hopped onto the sidewalk. Kathryn led the way to the entrance of the town hall.

"How are we going to do this?" I asked. "What's our plan?"

"I'm not sure yet. I'm going to wing it. Maybe someone will be kind and help us, guide us in our search."

I smiled at Kathryn. I was grateful she had so much interest in helping me. I thought perhaps that she had some interest in Charles as well. They seemed very friendly today.

"I believe Charles thinks highly of you, Kathryn," I said. "He's always looking toward you, waiting for your approval or something."

Kathryn smiled. "You suppose?"

"Yeah, I do."

Kathryn sighed. "I don't know why but I feel compelled to help him. He seemed so sad when you talked about Jack. I really don't mind spending time with him either. I just get all confused. My life is really complicated sometimes."

I gave her a weird look like, *Come on, what is so hard about your life?*

"Don't look at me that way. You don't know everything."

"Well, you can always talk to me. I won't judge. I'll listen and give you my best solid advice, if you want it."

Kathryn laughed. "What do you know? You're barely out of high school."

"I know when two people have affection for each other and I think Charles has affection for you."

"Maybe he's just feeling vulnerable."

"Maybe. Maybe not."

"I'm involved with someone, Lucy. That makes it complicated."

"You have a boyfriend? Demetry?" I asked again, eyeing down my sister as we spoke.

"*No way!*" Kat said, laughing. "Demetry is not my boyfriend!" She looked at me and rolled her eyes. "Anyway, just forget it for now, I don't really want to get into depth about it."

"Okay, Kat. Let's ask this lady where the town clerk is." I stepped up to her. "Excuse me, ma'am? We are looking for the town clerk's office. Could you point us in the right direction?"

"I'm heading there right now. You two ladies can follow me," she answered.

"Great, thank you," I said gratefully.

We were quiet as we walked the long hallway to the clerk's office. You could hear the woman's high-heeled shoes clicking on the floor as we made our way down. As we entered the office, there were several people waiting in line in front of us. "This is going to be awhile," I whispered. We sat on the bench and waited our turn. Finally, the woman behind the desk waved for us to come to her. Kat and I stood and approached her, nervously.

"How can I help you ladies?"

Kat started, "This is going to sound strange, ma'am, but we are looking for someone and we're not sure where to start."

The woman behind the desk was an elderly woman with kind eyes. She looked at us both up and down and gave a big sigh. "Who are you looking for?"

"Well, a neighbor of ours died several years ago, and her son was placed with a relative. We are trying to locate that relative."

I stood next to Kat while she did the talking. The old woman nodded as she was trying to figure out what it was we were looking for.

"Someone died? I could help you with that. Do you want a copy of the death certificate?"

I looked at Kat and smiled and nodded yes.

"It will cost you $5.00," the clerk added. Kathryn reached into her pocket and pulled out a $5 dollar bill.

"Thank you."

"Write down the name of the deceased person please, correct spelling." The town clerk passed a piece of paper and pen toward us. Kat wrote *Donna Nimchak* on the page. The clerk took the paper into the back room. When she returned she handed us a copy of the death certificate.

"Is there anything else you need?" she asked.

Kathryn already turned and was walking out of the office door.

"No. I think this is all we need. Thank you," I said as I hurried to catch up to her. "Is there any information, Kat?"

She turned and looked at me. "There's a birthplace!" Kat said excitedly. "Danville, Indiana!"

CHAPTER 32

Mama

Mama woke up that morning to the annoying noise of Mikey screaming at his sisters. She lay in bed and listened to them fight, arguing about who was going to clean the mess that Mikey had made, and Kaylan accurately accusing Mikey of thinking that it was his sister's responsibilities to keep cleaning up after him.

Mama continued to lie in bed, her sense of unease growing inside her. She thought about the day that was in store for her. She thought about the endless list of errands that she had and the ungrateful attitude her children had toward her. Negative, consistent thoughts invaded her mind as she lay still. Her children hated her; they must, how else could she explain how they treated her? They had no respect for her. They took advantage of her kindness and willingness to do anything for them. They needed her to do things for them, but they really didn't need *her*.

They didn't love her.

Mama slowly moved her legs out from under her covers and placed her feet onto the floor. Her face crumbled slightly as she tried to put her feet into her slippers. They evaded her as she fumbled around carelessly, trying to grab them with her toes. She started to cry, overwhelmed by her frustration. Today was not going to be a good day, she just knew it. Even her slippers were uncooperative.

She stood and walked into the hallway, startled suddenly by the mess Mikey had previously thrown on the floor in front of her: an emptied box of Lego parts strewn along the hallway, along with a toppled glass of apple juice and a pillow and blanket. Mama closed her eyes and counted to ten. She could feel the anxiety flush throughout her body as a blanket of heat seemed to be moving up her chest, into her arms, and around her neck. Frustration and anger continued to build in her throat as she moved forward, quickly deciding that her children weren't going to get away with this. She wasn't going to tolerate their behavior today.

"You damn fucking kids! Look at this mess. Who the hell made this mess and left it for me to clean? There's juice spilled fucking everywhere!" Mama screamed. Kaylan ran down the hall in front of her, a look of helpfulness mixed with nervousness spreading across her face.

"What, Mom?" Kaylan looked up at her mother. "Why are you swearing?"

"Who made this mess?" Mama turned to Kaylan, her face determined and angry.

"I don't know. Do you want me to clean it for you?" Kaylan asked, nervously picking up the toy pieces. Mama pushed past her, ignoring her and making her way for the stairs, her anger pressing her forward, eager to locate her son. She stomped up the stairs, yelling for Mikey. She continued to open and close the doors, screaming and slamming them shut. She could feel her body move as the anger had taken over, but she was unable to stop herself from losing control.

She could hear Mikey walking into the house from the outdoors, his big mouth nauseating her thoughts as she quickly made her way back down the stairs.

"Mikey, Mama is looking for you and she's pissed!" Kaylan whispered.

"So?"

"Did you spill juice on the floor this morning and leave it?"

"Uh, I don't think so, maybe I did? I don't know, big deal anyway."

"It is a big deal. It's rude for one and you know Mom can't handle any stress lately. Dad has already talked to you about this. I'm telling Dad when he gets home!"

Mama arrived in the kitchen and looked at Mikey, her face red with anger. "You little asshole. Did you deliberately spill your juice and leave it for me to clean up? What the hell is wrong with you?"

"There's no need to be upset, Mom; I'll clean it up," he said.

"I already cleaned it," Kaylan said carefully.

Mama grabbed Mikey by the arm. "I'm sick and tired of you. You're nothing but a nuisance." Mama's voice crackled as her words began to climb higher and higher. She felt like a bobcat running after her prey, ready to hunt it down and destroy it. She hollered until she no longer understood what she was saying. She grabbed Mikey and dragged him up the stairs, shrieking the entire time, swearing and berating him, not making any sense. Mikey started to fight back, kicking at her and punching her but she knew that she was stronger than him. She continued to smack him in his face and pulled his hair. "You be still, you little asshole. I just might kill you," she seethed through her teeth.

Mama dragged Mikey into his bedroom and threw him onto his bed, then locked his door from the outside. Satisfaction and relief washed over her. She convinced herself that this was how it needed to be. Her behavior was necessary and warranted, and there was nothing wrong with what she was doing. Mikey banged on the door and begged her to let him out. Mama started pacing the upstairs hallway and frantically began to yell some more.

"KAYLAN! KAYLAN!"

"Yes, Mama?" Kaylan asked nervously, appearing around the corner and watching warily as her mother banged down the stairway. Mama grabbed Kaylan's arm and started to drag her up the stairs. "What did I do?" she squealed. Mama started to cry, tears coming down her face. She knew her words were jumbled, her angry words not making sense. She knew that she was beyond stopping now, that she couldn't control herself. She was grateful that Kaylan knew better than to fight her. She was grateful that Kaylan was making it easier on her.

Mama dragged her into her bedroom and threw her to the floor. She locked the door as she left. She could hear Kaylan crying, praying for Jessica. Where was Jessica, how dare she hide from her? She began screaming her name once again, looking for her, running up and down the stairs, threatening her and searching for her throughout the house.

Mama found herself back in her room, an hour later, as she sat on her bed, staring at the wall. Forgetting about her children that she locked in their bedrooms, forgetting about Jessica who seemed to have successfully and smartly evaded her. Her mind becoming stilled and quiet, silence settling in as she slowly started to fall asleep exhausted by her fit of rage and resting her sick and tormented mind softly on her pillow.

CHAPTER 33

Lucy

Kathryn and I made our way back to Demetry's house. We were pretty excited to find where Donna Nimchak was born. "Maybe once we tell Charles the information we found, it will trigger a memory or two," I said to Kathryn. We were all sitting at the small table in Demetry's kitchen. Demetry was sitting back in his chair, listening to us tell him all about the great detective work we were both so proud of.

"So, let me ask you two something," Demetry said. "Now that you know where Mrs. Nimchak came from and where perhaps Jack Nimchak is living, how do you plan to get there?"

"I don't know. I haven't thought about that," I answered. I looked at Kathryn and I could tell that she was flustered. Perhaps she was thinking about the number of options that we might have, currently *none*. Kathryn looked up at Demetry.

"Couldn't you take us on a road trip, Dem?"

"No way, Kat. Don't think for one second that I'm getting involved in this great big adventure."

Kat looked at Demetry, disappointed. "You're off the hook, Dem, for now. Just pray we can find another way."

Demetry smiled at Kathryn.

"Well, if *you* had a car...."

"I know! Maybe we could borrow a car?" Kathryn said excitedly.

"Does Charles have a car?" I asked.

Suddenly I heard Charles: "Nope. No car here." Charles entered the room smiling at us all. "Hey Charles," Kathryn said, seemingly suddenly self-conscious.

"Demetry, this is Charles. Charles, Demetry." Demetry stood and reached out his hand.

"Nice to meet you," Charles said casually, accepting the handshake.

Charles looked at Kathryn. "What do we need a car for?"

"Here, sit down Charles. Let me get you a plate of food." Kathryn stood and hustled around the kitchen. I smiled to myself. It was nice to see Kathryn act so nervous around a boy.

"We have some information Charles," I said.

"Really? That's great! What is it?" Charles asked. Kathryn placed the plate of food in front of him. "Thank you, Kathryn. This looks fabulous."

I couldn't wait to tell Charles the information. "Well, we managed to get a copy of your mother's death certificate. On the copy it states her birthplace—Danville, Indiana."

Charles looked up at me. "Indiana?" he asked, suddenly defeated. "This is going to be impossible. Indiana is in the middle of the country. How on earth will we ever get there?"

Kathryn added, "That's why we need a car."

"Oh, I see. So, you want to drive there?" Charles put his head down, took a fork, and began to eat his supper.

"Have you ever heard of Danville, Indiana? Does that town ring a bell?" I asked.

Charles shook his head no. "I don't ever remember hearing of Indiana."

"Do you think your grandfather could be there?" I asked.

Demetry chimed in. "There's a lot of farmland in Indiana."

"There's a chance he could be anywhere," Charles objected.

"Well, there's only one way to find out. We need to go there," I said. Everyone in the room looked at me. "Give me a day or two. I'll find a way," I said with confidence. I stood from my chair. "I need to get home, Kathryn. I haven't been home all day."

"Yeah, okay. Tell Mom I'll stop by tomorrow."

I gave Kathryn a hug. "Thank you, Kathryn, for everything."

Charles stood and kissed me awkwardly on my cheek.

"Thank you, Lucy. You've been a huge help," Charles said.

I smiled at him. "You're welcome."

The short walk home was refreshing and tiring. I couldn't wait to go to bed. It dawned on me that I forgot to call Amelia. I wanted to tell her about Jack. I guess I could call her in the morning.

As I approached the house, I noticed Julia's car was in the driveway. *Why is Julia home?* I thought. *She never comes home during the week.*

I walked up the porch and into the side entrance door to the kitchen. Julia was standing there, finishing the dinner dishes. "Hey Jules, what are you doing here?" Julia looked at me, her eyes full of concern and worry.

"Dad called me home. There's something going on with Mom." I sat down at a stool in the kitchen, giving Julia my attention as she spoke, my heart feeling pangs of guilt and regret for having left her alone all day. I knew she needed my help.

"Did she get hurt?" I asked.

"No, it's much worse. Have you noticed anything strange about Mom lately?"

I put my hands in my lap and I thought about my mother and all her odd behavior over the last few months. "Yeah, well, I think she's under a lot of stress."

"Well, she locked Kaylan and Mikey in their rooms today, all day long. I guess she got upset over spilt juice and went a little crazy. Kaylan said she was saying things and she wasn't making any sense."

I stared at Julia not believing what she was saying. I jumped off my stool and ran for the stairs. "Where's Kaylan and Mikey? Are they okay? I need to see them."

Julia tried to calm me down. I heard her voice telling me to stop, but I was already halfway up the stairs. I needed to see for myself. I reached Kaylan's bedroom and threw open the door, startling them as they sat playing a game of Monopoly. Kaylan looked up at me and gave me a silly smile. She jumped and ran over to hug me.

"You're home!" she said.

"I'm home. I'm so sorry I left you guys. Is everyone okay?" I asked, kissing Jessica and Mikey on their faces.

"We're fine. Mom went to Grandma's. Dad took her."

I took a deep breath.

Julia finally made it up the stairs. "Dad thought it would be a good idea if she had a break from everyone for a few days. Let her clear her head."

"So, that's why Dad called you?" I asked.

"Yes, I'm going to stay here and help out."

"I could take care of the kids," I offered.

"I know you can, Lucy, but I have a few days off. We can do this together, while Mom is gone. Okay?"

"Yeah. Okay." I looked around the room and at my siblings. They seemed happy and content playing their game.

Julia nodded at me. "Can we talk?"

My heart was calmer but I still needed to know more about the situation. "Yeah, let's go downstairs." I followed Julia back into the kitchen and sat down on my stool.

"Dad's really worried about Mom. He thinks she needs to be in psychiatric care."

"*What?!* Like she's really going crazy?"

"Yes. Lucy…something's not right. She's never hit any of us kids her whole life. She's swearing and flying off the handle."

I focused and silently agreed with Julia. "She came into my room the other night and stared at me. She never said anything; she just stood there and then turned and left. Freaked me out. So weird. When I asked her about it, she pretended to remember, but I don't think she did."

Julia sat finally and shook her head, back and forth. "It's so hard to understand."

"Well, maybe Grandma could help her."

"Let's hope so, Luce. Someone has to help her." Julia stood and headed for the stairs. "I'm going to put the twerps to bed. You look tired too. Why don't you go and relax in your room. Everything is fine and under control for now. Go get some rest."

I followed Julia upstairs toward my bedroom. I was very tired. Today was a crazy day full of so much emotion. Now my mother? Tomorrow's a new day. *I'll figure it all out tomorrow,* I told myself as I fell asleep on my bed.

CHAPTER 34

Lucy

The next day I awoke to Amelia sitting on my bed.

"Amelia!" I said sleepily. What are you doing here?"

Amelia threw a pillow at me. "Waking you up, silly. I waited all day yesterday to hear from you. What's going on with you? You never not call me."

I pulled my blankets over my head, the thoughts of yesterday all coming back to me. "I was really distracted yesterday. So much is going on. I don't even know where to start."

Amelia pulled the covers back off my face. "I can't understand you if you're going to talk through the blankets."

I sat up and started to tell Amelia the long story about Jack. She sat listening, attentive to every word I was saying. I then proceeded to tell her about my mother. By the end of the conversation, Amelia picked up the blankets and threw them back over my head. She laughed, "No wonder you didn't have time to call me. Geez, Lucy!"

"I know, so that's the story. I'm really torn. I want to keep looking for Jack, but I can't leave my family now. Everyone needs me." I stood and grabbed my bathrobe.

"It sounds like your mother is in good hands, and Julia's home, so I *know* your family is going to be okay," Amelia said in her soothing voice.

I looked at Amelia and agreed with her. *She's nervous,* I thought to myself.

"What's up with you? Why are you acting weird?" I asked.

"I came here to tell you some news, but now I feel like it's inappropriate considering everything else you have going on."

I sat down next to Amelia and put my arm around her shoulder. "I always have time for you, Amelia. You can talk to me."

"You're not going to like what I have to say."

I stared at Amelia. I paused for a moment and said, "You're dating my brother?!"

Amelia stared at me with her mouth open wide. "How did you know?"

"It's obvious and my brother's been in love with you for years. I figured it was just a matter of time."

"So, you're not angry?"

"I don't know what it is you see in him," I laughed, "but I'm not angry." I had known deep down inside that Thomas and Amelia were eventually going to find each other. It was hard to ignore the looks that they shared, the giggling and the flirtation as they communicated. He loved her; I knew that I wasn't going to be able to stop them. Besides, I needed to focus my energy on Jack and my mother. I couldn't worry about something that I had no control over.

Amelia threw her arms around me and hugged me. "I've been so worried about this moment. It's such a relief. You know how much I love you."

"Maybe we'll be real sisters one day," I said as I grabbed a towel for my shower.

"Oh my god, Lucy! Could you imagine? That's like a dream come true!" Amelia sat on my bed with a silly grin on her face. "By the way, Tommy has a car. Did you forget about that? Maybe he could help you find Jack."

I looked back at her, suddenly very grateful for her and Tommy's relationship. "I didn't consider Tommy, but maybe now if *you* asked him...maybe he would say yes!"

Amelia stood and walked toward the door. "I'll handle it, Lucy. I owe you one. Let me work on him."

"That would be the best, Amelia. Good luck! Call me later." I walked into the bathroom and stood under the showerhead for thirty minutes. I had to figure this out. Could I leave my mother? I needed to talk to my dad. Maybe Tommy would take us. It could be fun. A road trip!

CHAPTER 35

Lucy

I found my father in the garage. His usual spot in the back, fixing an old wooden desk.

"Hey, Dad!" I said nervously.

"Hi honey, how are you dear?" My father looked up from his handiwork to smile at me.

"I'm good, Dad. Do you have a minute?"

My father put down his tools and waved me to come closer to him. "Of course I do."

"You remember Charles and Jack Nimchak, don't you?"

"Yeah sure, the two young boys, their poor mother."

I started to pace a little. "Charles has come back into town and he's looking for his brother, Jack."

My father looked up at me. He moved his head slightly, urging me to continue.

"Kathryn and I have been trying to help him. We think Jack might be in Danville, Indiana. That's where his mother was born and where his grandfather may still live."

"Really? I always wondered whatever became of those two boys. Well, I think it's very kind of you and Kathryn to help those poor kids."

The next question was so hard. How do you leave your family when they are in the middle of a crisis? So much guilt. I pressed forward.

"We'd like to take a trip to Indiana, to see if we could find Jack."

My father glanced at me, confused, tired, and annoyed now. He rose and returned to his woodworking.

"Who are these 'we' you're speaking of?"

"Well, Tommy has agreed to drive us, if it's okay with you. Charles, of course, Kathryn, and Amelia."

My father sighed. "I would never agree to this, Lucy, but with your mother and the circumstances that we're facing, I'm almost compelled to say yes."

I jumped up, excited. "Really?"

My dad tried to calm me down. "Not that I like it, Lucy, but I think it might be easier with fewer people in the house. Your mother should be coming home soon; it may be less stressful."

I ran to my father and gave him a hug. "Thank you, Dad! It's real important to me."

"I can see this."

"Julia says she's staying for a few weeks," I added, trying to soften my own guilt for leaving.

"Yes, I know. We will be fine. I hope you find Jack," Dad said. "I love you, honey."

"I love you too, Dad." I turned to leave, trying to contain the excitement I felt running through my arms as I thought about seeing Jack again. "Thank you, Dad!" I yelled again from the driveway.

"You're welcome!" My father sat back in his chair, shaking his head.

CHAPTER 36

Jack

The dreams haven't stopped. Every night is the same. I dream of Lucy and of someone trying to kill me. It's infuriating. Sometimes I'm able to take my frustration out on the football field. It feels good to really hit someone. Hit them hard.

I wish I'd killed my mother's murderer. I visualized punching him in his face and knocking his teeth out. I pictured myself looking at him on the ground while he struggled to breathe, and I envisioned watching him die. Eventually he lays there, dead. I tried to shake these bad thoughts out of my head. It was no good to be angry. So many positive things had happened to me since my mother's death. I tried to be grateful, but it was hard to stay focused on the here and now.

I walked into the kitchen and sat with Pop at the table.

"How are you, Jack?"

"I'm good, Pop. Hungry!" I grabbed some eggs and bacon and stood to get a cup of coffee.

"That darn heifer went loose again last night. She's up grazing at Nelson's upper field."

"Do you want me to round her up for you?"

Pop smiled at me. "That would be great. Have breakfast first. You're practically a man now; you need to eat."

I laughed. "You don't have to tell me twice. I'm starving."

Susie Mae walked into the kitchen humming a sweet tune with a pretty smile on her face. "From the looks of it, I don't think I need to ask, 'How's breakfast?'" She stopped to kiss my cheek and patted me on the shoulder.

"You know I enjoy everything you cook, Susie!"

"Mhmm."

"What field do you want the cow in, Pop?" I placed my finished plate into the sink as I stood to leave.

"Bring her down here, in the lower pen. I need to keep an eye on her. She's the only wanderer I have."

"Okay. I'll be back in a jiffy. Thanks, Susie!"

"You're welcome."

I grabbed my old weathered cowboy hat I stole from Pop when I first arrived on the farm. It must be a hundred years old. It's worn in all the right places and it fits me just right. Pop has tried to take it from me several times; he's even tried to give me a new one. But I like this one, it's special to me. It looks like how I felt when I first arrived here—beaten and battered. I don't ever want to forget those days.

As I walked down to the barn, I could hear the horses; they all wanted to get out for a run. I looked at the large red barn before me. The steel weathervane on its peak moving slightly in the wind, the light green patina on its metal shimmering in the sunlight. I walked past the white picket fence horse pen, the eight-foot tall sunflowers standing strong on either side of the entrance, a mare and her baby strolling along the inner circle. I looked up the hill toward the rows of apple trees in the distance. The orchards that appeared like a checker table, one after the other, lines and rows of neatly manicured trees. I looked forward to riding today. Who would be the lucky star, I thought. I knew I had to go with my baby. "Ginger Sweet" I called her. She was a beautiful mare, strong and solid. Her red coloring and her white mane and kneecaps made her incredibly special.

She heard me coming and poked her head out of her stall. "Hey baby," I said to her. I placed my hand on her face and she put her head on my shoulder as if to hug me. "Do you want to go for a ride?" Her head jerked up and she stepped to the back of her pen so I could open her gate. "You're so smart, Ging."

I took her leash and strapped on her mouthpiece. I kept her in the walkway of the barn so I could brush her and clean her horseshoes. She loved to be groomed. Spoiled. For her sweet and well-behaved attitude, I gave her an apple. I threw on her blanket and then her saddle. We walked out of the barn and she pulled from me carefully so she could prance around. She enjoyed giving the other animals a little show. I laughed to myself. Who knew these animals had so much personality? It was amazing.

"Okay, Ginger, are you through? Can we go now?" I asked. She approached me slowly and waited as I mounted her with ease and elegance.

"HEE-YA!" I yelled, and off we went. Ginger ran at a fierce speed out of the barnyard, beyond the pasture of hay grass, and over the hill of apple orchards until we hit the wood line.

"You should have been in the races," I told her as I leaned into the back of her neck. I loved riding. My mind was focused only on the view of the land and the animal I was riding on. It was so peaceful. So relaxing. I turned back and looked at the farm behind me, the white farmhouse appearing smaller as we rode forward, a flock of ducks flying from the lower pond and out into the dark blue sky above me.

"Okay, Ginger. Keep your eye out for that crazy cow."

We trotted gracefully through the wooded section of the farm, up past Nelson's house and finally to the upper fields.

I spotted the calf right away. I could hear her mooing and crying, a sure sign of distress. I clicked my heels and urged Ginger to gallop toward the animal. She quickly bolted and approached the injured cow.

"Oh boy, what did you do to yourself here?" I jumped off Ginger and grabbed another apple out of my pocket to give to the cow. I petted her large head to comfort and ease her. It looked like her hoof got caught in some barbed wire. I bent down to look at it. I removed the wire around her ankle and took my handkerchief and wrapped the wound. "This should get you home, little wanderer."

Mr. Nelson was waving at me from his front porch. I waved back to assure him that everything was okay and that I didn't need his help. As he was waving I saw Angie trotting toward us on her horse. Angie was Mr. Nelson's daughter. Pop always talked about her, what a nice girl she was. He was right, of course. She was a very attractive girl. She was strong, knowledgeable, and very smart. We sat next to each other in senior math class.

Ginger started to make some noise, feeling threatened as Angie approached us with her horse. I grabbed onto

Ginger's rein and tied it to the wooden fence running along the hillside. I grabbed Angie's horse, helped her down, and then tied her horse up the same.

"Thanks, Jack," Angie said. "What's happening here?"

"Oh, this old heifer got caught up in some wire. I wrapped her wound. I think she'll be alright once I get her back home."

"Do you mind if I take a look?"

"Yeah, sure, go ahead."

Angie quietly walked over to the cow and reassured it that she wasn't going to hurt her. She kneeled and picked up her hoof.

"Jack, grab my bag off my horse. I have a few medicinal items in there. I'll give her a proper dressing, that way she'll make it home no problem." I knelt down beside Angie and took a better look.

"You don't like my veterinary skills?" I said as I laughed. I stood back and grabbed her bag.

"Well, with what you had available, I'd say you did a fine job." Angie looked up at me smiling. She quickly turned her eyes away from mine. She's cute when she's shy. I watched Angie dress the heifer's hoof. She was gentle and sweet. The animal never flinched.

230

Angie pulled back her wavy, dark hair and layered it on top of her head so it didn't fall into her face. The curly auburn tendrils escaped wherever they could. I watched her intently. I suddenly became very aware of every single movement she made. The way her breasts looked in her shirt, so tight and snug and full. I was aware of her ragged jeans clinging to her ass and the way her muck boots formed so nicely around her calves. She truly was an attractive girl. I grabbed her hand to help her stand and pulled her quickly against me, unintentionally, but happy to get a good smell of her skin. She took a step back, embarrassed.

"I'm sorry, Angie, that was my fault. Don't know my own strength."

Angie smiled timidly. "That's alright, you're a strong boy."

"Hey, thanks for taking care of that wound," I said quickly to change the subject.

Angie walked back to her horse and placed her bag on her saddle. "Yeah, no problem. I hate to see an injured animal. It breaks my heart."

"I know what you're saying; these animals have so much personality."

Angie looked at me with enthusiasm. I could see the passion in her eyes when she talked about animals. "Don't they? Animals could be so funny sometimes. I really get attached to my little beasts."

"You should be a vet, Angie. You would be an excellent doctor."

"I've thought about it. It's hard to imagine going away to school somewhere. My dad relies on me here on the farm."

She was saying the words that I'd thought so many times. How do you leave your family when they need you? "I'm sure your father wants the best for you, Angie. You would come back once you've finished your schooling, wouldn't you?"

"Yeah, I would. Dad wants me to do it. He says our town needs a decent vet. Mr. Jenkins is old and will be retiring someday."

I walked toward Angie as she was trying to mount her mare. "Do you mind?" I asked as I offered my hand to give her a boost.

She smiled and put her foot in my hand as I hoisted her up in her saddle. I allowed my hand to rest on her thigh as she situated herself.

"Thank you, Jack. It's always nice talking to you."

"Don't be such a stranger, Angie. I live right down the road if you or your father ever need anything." I untied her mare and handed her the reins.

She turned her horse around and looked back at me one last time. She smiled. She's beautiful. "Hee-ya! She hollered and quickly rode out of my sight.

I hopped up on Ginger and we slowly got the cow back down the hill toward our farm. I thought about Angie the entire time. Maybe Pop was right. Maybe it was time to get involved and date a little. See what happens.

Pop was eagerly waiting for me when I entered the barnyard with the wounded animal. "I was afraid of this," he said.

"Sorry it took so long, Pop. It was slow going."

"I bet it was. Well done, Jack! You did a fantastic job. It's very difficult to handle an injured animal. They can become very stubborn."

"Well, I ran into Angie Nelson. She was very helpful. She took care of the wound for me."

"Oh, Angie?" Pop said with a suspicious tone while eyeing me down. I smiled at him.

"She's pretty cute, Pop."

Pop beamed with pride. "Well, I'm happy to have her home. Thank you."

"You're welcome. I'm going to head to practice now. I'll see you later."

"Okay, Jack. Good luck, son."

I walked back to our house to grab my things. Angie Nelson. Yes, she's definitely cute.

CHAPTER 37

Lucy

Our road trip was planned, mapped and we were ready to go. It was a Saturday morning. I lightly packed a small bag and said goodbye to my siblings. I thanked Julia for staying and helping out and apologized for leaving her in the midst of all that has happened.

"Just go, already. You think you're the queen of everything. We *can* survive without you, Lucy!"

I hugged her again. "You're the best, Julia. I'll never forget this!"

Tommy and Amelia sat in his car in the driveway. He eagerly beeped his horn and was yelling for me. "Let's go already, Luce! Geez!"

I ran down the steps of the porch and threw my bag into the trunk of the car. Dad came out and gave us a final goodbye. He bent down in Thomas' window and offered him some final words of advice, driving tips, and route suggestions should we get lost. We waved goodbye and pulled out of the driveway. I was so nervous and excited that I could hardly sit still in my seat.

Amelia turned to me. "This is going to be so much fun, Lucy. I'm so happy to be a part of it."

Thomas looked at Amelia. "Are you going to talk to her the entire trip like this? Sit straight and put your seatbelt on. I don't want anything happening to you."

Amelia reached over and gave him a big kiss on his cheek. "You're so protective!" she said sarcastically.

I sat up and put my head in between the two of them in the front seat. "Is it better like this, Tommy?" I asked, laughing. "Do you want me to do this instead, the entire trip?"

"No thanks!" Tommy said, annoyed.

Amelia and I giggled.

"You girls are silly. I think Charles will have to sit in the front with me while you girls can all sit in the back."

"Perfect!" Amelia said, pleased with the arrangements.

We pulled into Demetry's driveway and beeped the horn. Amelia jumped into the back seat, flailing her butt and legs into the air. She took her place next to mine. She grabbed onto my arm and whispered in my ear, "Are you dying yet?"

I shook my head no and smiled at her and covered my eyes. "I just can't stand it, I'm so excited," I said. I wasn't sure what I'd do if we got to Indiana and there was no Jack. I couldn't even consider it.

Kathryn exited her house and threw her bags into the trunk. Charles was two feet behind her.

"Hey Charles, sit up front with me," Thomas suggested. Charles smiled at Tommy and hopped into the front seat. He turned and said hello to Amelia and me. He looked at me. "I'm so nervous, Lucy. What if we don't find him?"

I rubbed his shoulder. "We will, Charles. We will."

Charles turned and looked out of the front window, a thoughtful look on his face.

"Are you ready, man?" Tommy asked.

"I really appreciate you helping us out, Tommy. I owe you big time," Charles responded.

I turned to Kathryn. She looked so stressed. "Are you okay, Kat?"

She glanced around at the street, distracted. "Yeah, I just want to get going. Can we leave already?"

Demetry opened the front door and stood on the stoop, waving. "Remember, don't call me!" he yelled from the porch.

Kathryn shot him an evil look.

"I love you, Dem," she responded out of her window, unconvincingly.

Just then a car pulled up. Kathryn looked behind her. "God damn it! Hold on guys, I'll be right back." Kathryn opened her door and approached the girl in the car.

"Who's that?" I asked.

"That's Samantha Barnett," Tommy answered. "She went to high school with Kathryn."

We all watched Kathryn as she spoke to Sam, her arms waving around angrily. Charles' eyes focused on only Kat as a concerned look crossed his face.

"What the hell is going on?" I asked. "Why are they fighting?"

"Not sure," Tommy answered.

"They probably got into a tiff," Amelia added. "You know how girls are."

I nodded, not quite understanding.

Tommy poked his head out of the window. "Wrap it up, girls!" He slowly pulled out of the driveway. Samantha was crying and grabbing onto Kathryn's arm. Kathryn looked stern and pissed off. She walked away from Sam and headed back to our car. She jumped into her seat.

"Just go," she said, irritated.

Tommy quickly put the car in drive and sped down the road, leaving Sam to herself. Kathryn turned to look at me. "*Don't* ask any questions!"

I was ready to speak, and then I slowly sat back in my seat and shut my mouth. It was quiet in the car for ten minutes, Kathryn, just staring out of her window.

Thomas pulled into the parking lot of the gas station. "We have to fuel up before we head out of town. Does anyone want any snacks before we go?"

Amelia and I offered to go inside and grab some food and drinks for everyone. Charles and Kathryn stayed behind.

When I exited the Cumberland Farms, I noticed Charles and Kathryn, embracing. I walked slowly, hoping to give them enough time to have their moment. I smiled to myself. It warmed my heart to see Kathryn involved with Charles. For some reason, I felt like she needed him. She seemed so lost, so confused about her life. I hoped that Charles would be a good influence and that they would be good for each other. I knocked on the window of the car and then opened the door. "Sorry, guys. They only had Diet Coke."

"Thank you, Lucy," Kathryn said as she sat back down in her seat. She looked at me out of the corner of her eye. A smile emerged. She looked like she was going to crack at any moment. Charles glanced back at her and smiled.

"This trip is going to be fantastic," Kathryn said.

I rolled my eyes. "Oh boy, looks like we have two sets of lovebirds now. I guess I'm the fifth wheel on this trip!" I teased.

Tommy and Amelia walked out of the store holding hands. They both got into the car. "What did we miss?" Amelia asked. Kathryn, Charles, and I started laughing.

"Nothing," I said, shaking my head.

Tommy started the car. "Off we go, people!"

"Hurray!" said Kathryn.

"Woo hoo!" I yelled as we pulled out of our first gas station.

CHAPTER 38

Julia

Julia prepared the kids' lunches for camp and then they all waited for the school bus at the corner. The bus came right on schedule. She kissed them all goodbye and waved as they pulled away. She knew her father was waiting for her. He wanted to talk to her about her mother. Her heart felt dreadful. Julia knew her mother was not doing well.

She walked back down the driveway into the house. Her dad was sitting, drinking his coffee.

"Kids are all set, Dad. Off to camp."

"Good, Julia." He looked up at her and took a deep breath. "I'm so thankful you are here, honey. I don't know how I would manage without you." He took a sip of his coffee.

"Thanks, Dad. So, what's the latest on Mom? Have you talked to Grandma?"

"It's so complicated, Julia. Your grandmother is definitely in denial over her illness. I spent two hours with Mom yesterday. She sat in a chair in her old bedroom and stared out of a window during the whole visit. I asked her if she wanted to come home. She looked at me, her eyes full of panic and fear. She shook her head no! I thought that if she had a break from the kids, I would see some improvement in her. I think it's getting worse."

Julia grabbed a cup of coffee for herself and sat down next to her father, overwhelmed by their conversation.

"What do you think should happen, Dad?"

"I think she needs serious mental help. I'd like to admit her for a psychiatric evaluation. Your grandmother is fighting me on it. She's so backwards. I asked her how she's eating, is she showering, does she go outside?" Her dad looked down at his empty cup of coffee. She could see the stress lines in his face, the sleepless nights of worry evident in his appearance and body language.

"You look tired, Dad," she murmured as she stood to give her father a hug.

"I need to convince your grandmother that *my wife, your mother* needs more care. She's not getting her to eat or care for herself. It's not working. Anyway, I've already spoken to the head of the psychiatric clinic, down at UConn Medical. He's an old friend from high school. He said he's willing to sit with her. He will ask her a series of questions and then perhaps he can give me some advice. I have an appointment tomorrow."

Julia sat there and listened. She listened to her father vent, talk, and complain about her grandmother. A single thought kept popping into her head: *She'll never get out of this place. She's going to be stuck here forever.*

She stood and started to clean the kitchen. "I think that's a great idea, Dad. What do you have to lose? It can't hurt for Mom to talk to someone. I think you're doing the right thing."

Her father stood and put his cup in the sink. "Thanks, Julia. I'm going to work now." He bent and kissed her on her cheek. "I'll see you tonight."

"Okay, Dad. Try to have a good day." Julia smiled and walked him to the door. She watched as her father pulled out of the driveway. She wished she could make it better for him. Better for everyone.

A sense of dread flooded her belly. She could feel it in her gut. Her mother was giving up, but she needed to fight for them. What words of encouragement could Julia say to her? She wished she could do it for her, give her the strength and courage. She wanted to beg her to be a badass. Fight! Fight!

She cleared her head and started back on doing her chores. She felt helpless. She couldn't *will* someone to want to live. If only she could control her mother, tell her what to do and guide her to better health. She could make it better for them. She could help her mother if she would just listen. She could make her eat and help get her strength back. She would convince her that her family needed her; that they were worth the fight.

Nobody listened to her.

CHAPTER 39

Jack

One more week of football and next weekend was the big game. Our small town carefully prepared itself for victory. The city officials had placed a huge billboard in the center of the green supporting our high school team. *"GO DANVILLE!"* it stated with balloons and flowers all around. All the teammates' names were posted along with our victories and losses. There's a big bonfire tonight. Already, the town had stacked wood pallets reaching fifteen feet high for the event. The excitement was in the air.

I drove home after practice. I needed to finish my chores early so I could meet up with some buddies before the fire. I passed Pop on the way and waved. He was out in the cornfield on one of the tilling machines, prepping the land for next year's planting. I pulled into the yard and saw Susie Mae, hanging some laundry. I waved. I could smell supper cooking.

My stomach growled as I walked into the kitchen. I opened the oven and pulled out a ham, and I grabbed a corner piece and popped it into my mouth.

"What are you doing, boy?!" Susie Mae hollered as she stood behind me, hands on her hip.

I jumped half a mile. "Oh my god, you scared me!"

"Shut that oven door right now!"

"I couldn't help myself, it smells so good."

"Sit down, I'll make you a plate," she suggested motherly.

"I can't. I need to finish up some chores. I want to leave early tonight for the bonfire."

"A lot of excitement over this game. How are you feeling about it, Jack?"

"Good, actually. I think we're going to crush them." I stopped and pulled off my shirt to throw on some work clothes.

"Look at yourself, Jack. That football is making you stronger than ever. So handsome, my boy."

I laughed at her. "Maybe if I shave once in a while."

"Eh, you're good looking even with the stubble. Girls go crazy for you, I'm sure," Susie Mae said as she handed me my work shirt.

"Yeah, I guess. I'm hoping to run into Angie Nelson tonight. Not sure if I will, but hoping."

"Oh, she's a sweet girl, Jack. I have a soft spot for Angie," Susie said thoughtfully. "Well, you run out and get your chores done. I'll fix up your clothes nice so you have something decent to wear. Make a good impression." Susie put her hand through my hair and messed it up like a little kid. "How about that nice linen shirt? The relaxed one, looks good with your old beat-up cowboy hat."

I grabbed Susie and gave her a big hug. She struggled to get away from me, laughing, but I wouldn't let her go. I gave her a big kiss and released her. "I love you, Susie Mae."

She beamed and blushed and pushed me out of the house. "Okay, okay, okay. Don't get all mushy. Its just laundry." She laughed.

I walked out of the house. I loved how she yelled at me, scolded me, and then mothered me. I would do anything for Susie Mae and Pop. They're just good people. I love it here.

CHAPTER 40

Lucy

After seven hours' driving in the car, we were all ready for a break. We made our way out of Pennsylvania and had traveled some good distance. "I'm starving. Anyone else hungry?" I asked.

"How about I pull over at the next exit, we'll stop for dinner," Tommy stated.

Charles agreed. "Sounds good."

Tommy pulled off the exit and headed west on Main Street, toward the center of town. "Boy, there's quite a gathering of people here," he said. We watched through the car windows as folks walked around, up and down the street.

"I wonder what's happening?" Tommy muttered.

I sat quietly staring out at the street. I was ready for a nap. Driving in the car all these hours had made me sleepy. I thought about Jack and imagined him driving out west with his grandfather and everything he must have seen and felt. I imagined that I was experiencing the same things he had. I wanted to remember everything.

"What's going on, Tommy?" Amelia asked.

Tommy slowed his car to a steady pace, as traffic seemed to be picking up as we entered town.

"Not sure. Seems to be some kind of parade or something. There must be somewhere decent to eat. Keep your eyes open."

"What's wrong with everyone?" Charles said. "These people seem pissed off at something."

"Yeah, I know. I think it's a protest."

"Cool. I love to protest. I wonder what the cause is," Kathryn said, finally interested.

Tommy pulled his car into a parking lot alongside the first diner we saw.

"Can't wait to stretch my legs," Amelia complained.

"I can't wait to use the restroom." I laughed.

"Oh my gosh, I've had to pee since New York," Amelia stated, always one for dramatics. Kathryn looked at me sideways and shook her head.

"Princess Amelia needs to use the bathroom, Tommy," Kathryn declared as she nudged Amelia out of the car. Amelia and Kathryn had never spent this much time together. *I think they like each other*, I realized. Amelia was just a little more high maintenance than Kathryn, but they seemed to be getting along. We made our way into the diner and headed straight for the bathroom.

"We'll grab a table," Charles yelled.

We walked into the bathroom and stopped short as we entered the dingy, dark space.

"Yuck! This is an awful mess," Amelia complained.

"Gross! If only I didn't have to go so bad. I would hold it until the next state!" Kat laughed.

"Well, hold your breath and make it quick," I said. Amelia gave me a wicked look, mortified that she had to use *this* bathroom. "Sorry, Amelia. I don't think we have a choice."

Kathryn quickly glanced at herself in the mirror. "Oh, god. Look at my hair."

"Since when do you care about your hair?" I asked suspiciously as I entered the stall. "Doesn't have anything to do with Charles, does it?" I yelled over the door.

"Let me help you, Kathryn." Amelia took off one of her hair ties and piled Kathryn's blonde, straight hair on top of her head. "That looks so cute, don't you think, Lucy?"

I was using the bathroom and trying to balance and not breathe while Amelia was asking me questions.

"Looks great, Amelia!"

"You can't even see it!" Amelia giggled. "What do you think, Kathryn? Do you like it? Here, try some of my lip gloss."

I flushed and opened the stall door. "That does look nice. You're so pretty, Kathryn," I said to my big sister.

"Okay, my turn." Kathryn hurriedly entered the second stall. "Oh my god, this is horrible!" she yelled.

We started to laugh. "Let's quickly do what we have to do and go look for the boys," I said eagerly.

We quickly finished and walked out of the ladies' bathroom to find Charles and Tommy.

"Wow, that was quick," Charles said to Kathryn.

"That was an unfortunate experience."

251

"That bad? The boys' room wasn't much better," Charles said in a low tone.

I sat next to Kathryn as Amelia sat next to Tommy. "Did you guys find out what's happening?" Amelia asked.

"Let's wait for the waitress; she probably knows." I picked up a menu and looked for something that caught my eye. "I think I'll get the BLT, fries, and a Coke," I said to no one in particular.

"That sounds really good, Lucy. I'll probably get the same," Amelia replied.

"I wonder if they have anything vegetarian," Kathryn asked.

Charles glanced at her with a bewildered look on his face. "You don't eat meat?"

"Nope!"

Charles smiled at her. "There's so much to learn."

Kathryn giggled and gave him a little shove.

Oh brother, I thought to myself.

The waitress finally made her way over. "Excuse me, ma'am? Is there some sort of protest going on?" Tommy asked.

The waitress snickered. "You kids from out of town?"

"Yes, ma'am. Just passing through on our way to Indiana."

The waitress looked at each and every one of us. "Well, the KKK is having a town forum on the center green today. Came through last night uninvited. Many people are upset, as you could imagine. We have a quiet, simple town here. You kids going to eat? What can I get you?"

Tommy looked up at the waitress, confused. "The KKK? Where the hell are we, the 50s? I've never heard of such a thing," Tommy exclaimed.

The waitress took our order. "Nothing surprises me anymore. You kids watch yourselves. Could get ugly out there," she warned as she turned to leave our table, shaking her head.

"We've got to check it out!" Kathryn stated.

"I don't know. I don't want to bring Lucy and Amelia around that shit," Tommy said fatherly.

"I can handle it, Tommy," Amelia protested. "Besides, you'll be with me the entire time." She placed her arm around him.

"It could be educational," Charles said sarcastically. He rolled his eyes at Tommy.

"I guess we could walk up the street. I don't want to stick around here too long; we still need to find lodging for the night."

I sat and ate quietly, thinking of Jack. I wondered if they had come through this town. I wondered if they sat in this diner. We finished our meals and asked for the check. Once we were on the street, we joined the opposing crowd walking toward the green. It was a mixed crowd of whites and blacks, young and old. People were shouting and hollering. Others carried signs that said, "*NOT IN OUR TOWN*" or "*EQUALITY FOR ALL.*"

My thoughts were confused and bewildered when we reached the town green. Eight men dressed in white robes with white headpieces. You couldn't see their faces. I'd seen pictures of the KKK, but never in person. One man was standing at a podium, speaking to the crowd, lecturing about the evils of mixing race and education. The crowd was arguing back and forth. None of it made sense. You couldn't really hear anything anyone had to say. It was all mumble-jumble.

Kathryn jumped up on a rock wall next to a large oak tree. She pulled Charles up next to her and they both started shouting their opinions.

"Arrogant fools!" Kathryn screamed.

"Damn haters!"

I took a seat in the grass up on a hill and watched it all unfold. Tommy took Amelia's hand and pulled her closer to the front so she could get a better view. There were angry people everywhere. I watched as a few men became physical, pushing and shoving each other. One man wore a blue factory work shirt, the kind my grandfather used to wear. He had a large belly, his shirt carelessly hanging over his pants. I thought to myself, *He should tuck his shirt in. He looks like a slob.* He and another man wearing the same kind of shirt were arguing and debating.

I watched the children interacting. The children had the right idea; they seemed to be ignoring the adults. There were kids playing marbles in the sand, some kids jumping rope in the grass. It was like the children didn't hear any of the fighting; they played with one another, black and white. They didn't care about the cause; they cared about playing.

One little girl caught my eye. She was standing alone and crying. She looked lost, and though there were adults all around her, none of them could seem to hear her. I quickly stood and made my way back down the hill. I pushed myself through the crowd until I reached the area where I thought I saw her. I looked around, but I failed to see where she went. I bent down into a crouched position and looked through the crowd of legs standing before me. There she was, sitting on the ground crying while the adults walked past and over her. I went to her quickly and picked her up, her three-year-old face nuzzled in my shoulder. I stood and waited for an adult, father or mother, anyone to approach me. I yelled into the crowd, "Is this anyone's child?" I looked at the little girl and wiped her cheeks. I gave her a reassuring hug and told her, "I will find your mommy. Are you here with your parents?"

She looked at me with big brown eyes. "My brother is here."

"Okay, sweetheart. Let's see if we can find a policeman to help us." I pushed my way back through the crowd to find a quieter, less populated area.

The police were present on the green. They stood in a line, trying to control the crowd. Black and white officers were working together. What an awkward scene. Like it or dislike it, people needed to learn patience. I could see Tommy and Amelia as they waved for me to come join them. I waved back. I bent down next to my little friend. "What's your name, honey?" I asked.

"Jessica," she stated shyly.

"Oh, I have a sister Jessica. I love that name. Can you tell me what your brother looks like?"

She looked up at me and shrugged her shoulders. I tried to remember Mikey when he was three. I tried to remember what he could communicate.

"Does he have a hat on?" I asked.

"No, he doesn't like hats," Jessica said in a little mouse voice.

I smiled at her. "How about a jacket? Does he like jackets?"

Jessica smiled. "Yes, he likes the Phillies. He wears his Phillies coat!" she exclaimed as she beamed with pride over her good answer.

"Okay. That is very helpful, Jessica. I am going to lift you up so you can help me look into the crowd and we are going to see if we can spot him anywhere."

Jessica lifted her arms toward me so I could pick her up. I placed Jessica on my hip and we both scanned the crowd eagerly looking for her brother. I could see Charles dragging Kathryn through the mob trying to reach Tommy and Amelia. Charles had his arm around her as he cleared the path for her to walk through. I looked further down at Tommy and Amelia. I tried to wave at them, to urge them to come back. I could see a police officer using mace on one of the protestors. Another officer had a different protestor on the ground and was placing handcuffs on him. This was getting out of control, I thought to myself. I suddenly had a very uneasy feeling spreading through my arms and chest. I looked around to find an escape route should I need one. The disorganized mob of people seemed to be getting larger.

Suddenly, I heard the voices of the crowd escalate in fear as a fire broke out in one of the garbage cans, catching on fire a light pole and bench along with it. The leader of the KKK, a man, was still speaking at the podium. I could tell he's uneducated. He didn't speak well. He spoke words of hatred, unintelligent words regarding ignorant and intolerant Negroes, sentences like, "we supposably going to accepts the collards," and "it reoccurred to me that Negros are a danger to me and my family." I shook my head at the ignorance and lack of education.

The crowd moved in waves. Protestors were shoving and pushing away from the fire toward the parking lot. "Oh god," I whispered. Jessica had her head on my shoulder. She felt heavy like she might fall asleep. Poor kid. I couldn't see my brother anymore. There was only one thing to do and that was to head back toward the car. We needed to get out of there.

Hopefully, I could find Jessica's stupid ass brother on my way, or at least a police officer. The chances of finding a police officer to help us would probably be difficult at this point. I took a deep breath as I felt anxiety fill my lungs. I carried Jessica tightly to my chest and I pushed back through the crowd toward the diner where we had eaten. I looked quickly for a Phillies jacket. I wasn't sure what I was looking for, but I hoped I'd recognize it when I saw it. *Maybe I could talk to the waitress again*, I thought, my mind spitting out ideas to cope with this situation. *She might be familiar with the family of this little sleeping girl I'm holding.*

A gentleman politely held the door for me as I approached the diner. As soon as I entered the building, I heard a boy, roughly around fourteen, exclaim in relief, "There she is!" *Dumb ass*, I thought. He stepped quickly toward me and grabbed Jessica out of my arms. Jessica took one look at him, smiled, and started to cry at the same time.

"Why did you leave me!?" she asked and slapped him in his face. I laughed at her reaction. Very appropriate, little one.

"I'm so sorry, Jessica. I turned for one minute and you were gone." Jessica's brother looked up at me with grateful eyes. "Thank you so much. What's your name?" he asked as he shook my hand.

"Lucy."

"Thank you so much, Lucy. Can I get you anything to eat, drink, anything? I'm so happy you found her and that she's safe. The crowd was getting unbearable and I was looking everywhere." His voice was shaky with panic.

"It's okay. I'm glad I found her too. I think you need to get her home. This is no place for a little girl her age," I said as politely as I could muster, considering what a jerk I thought he was.

"Absolutely, we're leaving right now. Thanks again. Say goodbye, Jessica, and thank you!"

Jessica bent down to give me a little kiss.

"Bye Jessica," I said, waving as they left the diner in a hurry.

I walked out just behind them and could see Charles and Kathryn approaching me quickly. "This demonstration is getting dangerous; we need to leave," Charles said. "It's a waste of time." Charles saw Tommy and waved to get his attention.

"Let's head back to the car," Kathryn said. "We'll meet them there."

"How much longer do you think, Charles? Till we reach Indiana?" I asked as we walked.

"I think if we drive a few more hours and then find somewhere to stop for the night, we'll only have about four hours in the morning."

I nodded my head. The reality of seeing Jack again was starting to set in. Tommy and Amelia finally made it back to the car.

"This was unbelievable!" Amelia said innocently.

"Could you imagine what it must have been like fifty years ago? You could feel the energy of the crowd, the anger and the passion," Kathryn stated thoughtfully.

"Are you okay, Lucy?" Amelia asked. "I was afraid we were going to lose you."

I placed my head on her shoulder. "That was scary," I said to her. She placed her hand in mine and we stayed like this. Tommy started the car and slowly pulled out of town.

"What a strange thing," I said as I looked out of the window at the town welcome sign. "That sign says, 'Welcome Friends! Peace, Love & Harmony.'" I chuckled quietly to myself. "I hope they find it," I mumbled under my breath.

CHAPTER 41

Julia

It was early Saturday morning. The phone was ringing. Julia pulled the blankets up over her head, thinking it was way too early. She heard the phone ringing again. She slowly dragged herself out of her warm, cozy covers. She walked into the hallway and met her father at the stairs.

"I've got it honey, go back to bed," he said to her.

Julia rolled her eyes and walked back into her room to collapse on her pillow. She'll never get back to sleep now, she thought to herself. She could hear her father on the phone. His voice was escalating. She worried that he would wake her younger siblings. She could hear him run up the stairs now and into her room.

"That was your grandmother! She doesn't know where your mother is! Hurry, get dressed!" he yelled, panicky.

"What do you mean, she doesn't know where she is? That's ridiculous. Where could she go?" she asked as she threw on her sweatpants. Her father ran back down the stairs. She quickly followed him as he put on his coat and grabbed his keys. "Where are you going, Dad?" she asked, her voice quivering. *This is bad.*

"I'm not sure, but I can't just sit here. I need to look for her."

Julia stood there as she watched her father run through the front door and into his car. She nervously walked toward the front living room to make some phone calls and she stopped.

It was her mother, lying on the couch.

"*Mom!*" she yelled. She quickly turned and ran out of the house to stop her father. He stopped his car and rolled down his window.

"What, Julia?!" he said, irritated.

"Mom's in the house, Dad!" she yelled. He quickly threw the car in reverse and parked it back in the driveway. They ran back into the house.

Her father approached her mother first. "She's freezing, Julia. Grab a blanket!"

Julia ran upstairs and grabbed two blankets and a pillow.

Her mother lay unmoving on the couch, but she was still alive. She mumbled words and moved her head back and forth as if she were experiencing a terrible dream.

"Mom, Mom, can you hear me?" Julia shook her and rubbed her to try to warm her.

"Look at her feet, Julia. She has no shoes," her father said, startled by his discovery.

"Oh my god," she said. Her mother's feet were blistered and swollen. She had scrapes and scratches and dried blood everywhere. "Dad, how did she get here? Do you think she walked from Grandma's?" Julia's grandmother lived five towns over. She would have walked all night in order to make it here in time for morning.

"Good god!"

"We need to call an ambulance," Julia said as she stood and grabbed the phone and dialed 911. She watched and spoke quietly to the operator as her father tried to wake her mother. Her mother was moaning and groaning, her words becoming clearer. She was asking for Lucy.

"Lucy's not here, Mama," Julia said to her.

"Where, where is she?" she asked, staring at her husband with blank eyes.

"She's away, on a trip, honey," he answered. "We're going to get you some help, darling. Stay with us, okay? Julia, grab her a robe; she's barely wearing any clothing. She's lucky she didn't freeze to death."

Julia ran back upstairs and did what her father asked. When she came back down, her mother was sitting up. Her eyes looked wild like an injured animal's.

She looked at Julia. "WHAT DID YOU DO TO LUCY?" she asked, her voice like the devil.

"Mom, relax. Lucy is fine. How did you get here, Mom?" Julia asked as calmly as she could, knowing her voice didn't sound calm.

"I WANT TO KNOW WHERE MY KIDS ARE. WHERE'S THOMAS?"

"Thomas is also on a trip. Lucy and Thomas are together. They are safe," Joseph said, rubbing her arms in attempt to calm her down.

Mama started to shake her head and cried, "YOU DID SOMETHING TO THEM, DIDN'T YOU? YOU NEVER LOVED THEM. YOU NEVER LOVED US!"

Julia looked at her father. He looked completely crushed.

"I would never hurt our children, honey. You're not yourself. You don't feel right. You're saying things that don't make sense." His voice cracked as he pled with his wife.

"I FEEL FINE, YOU SON OF A BITCH!" Mama stood, her voice terrifying as she lunged at Joseph in a fit of rage. She started to hit and scratch at his face, pulling his shirt away from his body.

"Mom!" Julia yelled as she tried to hold her back. She could lift her and swing her around with little effort, she'd lost so much weight. Her nightgown hung loosely on her body, revealing her bones and frailty.

The front door opened. Julia yelled, "In here!" as she held her mother down away from her father. Her mother continued to kick and scream and yell obscenities.

The EMTs entered the room and quickly sedated her so they could get her on the gurney. Julia stood back and watched them handle her mother. She tried so hard to cover her exposed figure, to put her robe on before they lay her down. Julia looked around the room and along the hallway to the kitchen. She could see her siblings standing against the walls, tears flowing from their eyes as the horrifying moment of watching their mother attack their father began to settle in.

She watched as her mother's behavior changed from wild and uncontrollable to lifeless and blank. Her mind numb once again, her eyes barely blinking. Julia went to her side and rubbed her face. "I love you, Mama," she whispered, but her mother didn't appear to have heard her words. The EMT's placed her mother into the ambulance and her father went with them.

"Call your grandmother," he said as he left.

Julia sat on the couch for a long moment before she could move again. Her hands shaking, her legs jelly. Her younger siblings began slowly circling in around her and next to her on the couch as they looked toward her for comfort. She needed to cry, but she couldn't. The shock of the situation was slowly settling in. It just seemed so unreal, so strange. How did this happen? She guessed it happened slowly. The signs had always been there, they just ignored them. Her mother needed help long before this. Her mother had lost her mind. Julia just prayed it wasn't too late.

CHAPTER 42

Jack

The night was warm and clear. I said goodnight to Pop and Susie and drove down town in my grandfather's beat-up pickup truck. I felt great. I was looking forward to hanging out with my friends. I wore my lucky cowboy hat just like Susie suggested. It felt right.

I took my time getting into town. I loved this time of day. The sun was setting and my windows were down, letting the warm air hit my face. The trees were in bloom. The countryside was blossoming and everything was green.

My grandfather's truck was rough around the edges but its antique mechanics and appearance made it a bit of a showpiece. It suited me fine and got me to school and back. I could hear it rattle as we made our way over the rugged roads of Danville. I waved at a few neighbors as I drove past St. Peter's Church and the Town Feed store. I pulled into the gravel parking lot at the town fairgrounds where the pep rally was taking place. They haven't started the bonfire; I suppose they were waiting until dark.

Families had spread blankets and children were running around here and there. I could hear the music playing as a small group of musicians have gathered on a stage and are playing guitar, singing and jamming to some old classics. I loved living in a small country town.

"Hey Jack!" a classmate yelled. I raised my hand and waved. Another townie approached me and shook my hand.

"Hey, Jack. Looking forward to seeing a great game next weekend, son."

"Thank you, sir, I plan to do my best. We've been working hard at practice and I'm confident we're going to crush them."

The man smiled and talked real close to my ear. "Kick their ASS, son!"

"Yes, sir! Will do!" I responded. I wasn't sure how this town would react should we lose the game next weekend. I continued to walk and could see some of my teammates gathered over by the bleachers, closer to the fire.

"Here he comes! Mr. Super Hero!" my buddy Aaron proclaimed. I laughed and reached out and gave him a man hug—partial handshake, partial chest pump. "How are you, man? We've been waiting for you!"

"I'm good!"

"We've started without you." Aaron handed me a nipper of brandy. A lot of my friends drank but for obvious reasons, I wasn't a big fan. Tonight I made an exception. I was feeling good and enjoying myself.

"Cheers," I said as I swigged the sweet brandy.

"Hey, there's a party down by the river later. We've got a keg on ice and the ladies are looking hot tonight. It's going to be a good time," Aaron said with a mischievous smile.

"Sounds cool, man. Count me in," I said. Aaron was like the male version of a party planner. He lived and breathed women and booze. I'd attended a few of Aaron's parties and I was always pretty impressed. There was good music, alcohol, and girls—lots and lots of girls.

I noticed my friend Adam, standing with the geek squad over by the cattle barn. I watched them as they talked animatedly to each other. They were probably discussing the possibility of some sort of human abduction tonight. I smiled to myself.

Someone had started the fire and the school principal and coach were standing at a podium with a microphone, hyping up the crowd. I stood tall with my hands in my pockets. I knew they were going to announce all the players; we were supposed to run up and high-five each other. I guess it would be good for the crowd. It was a feel-good kind of night. My buddy Lionel slapped me on the back.

"You ready, big boy? Ready to receive love from the people?" Lionel turned and ran when he heard his name called. He made his way over to the coach and started a receiving line to the left. I felt a little anxiety and a little embarrassment. I wasn't used to all this attention.

"Please give a round of applause for our starting quarterback, a true gentleman and absolute stellar athlete, JACK NIMCHAK!"

I slowly started my jog toward my teammates and coach.

"WOOHOO!"

"GET 'EM, JACK!"

The crowd was clapping and cheering. I turned and smiled, feeling important while all the eyes were on me. I scanned the crowd. It was quite a large gathering. I saw her— Angie. My heart jumped a little. She smiled at me and she gave me a tiny wave. I took my hat off and bowed slightly in her direction.

As soon as the coach was finished, my teammates started to disperse and head back to the bleachers. Angie stood and we walked toward each other. She looked so country, so naturally beautiful. "Hey Angie," I said. I felt a little awkward, like we had a secret that we shared, but we didn't.

"Hey big time," she said with a smile. I laughed, aware of how foolish I must have looked.

"Sorry about that. I had to take one for the team."

"Nah, you did great. There's a lot of good energy here tonight. I'm actually tempted to go watch the game next Saturday. I don't want to miss it," she said as she glanced at me.

"Yeah? You should come. Maybe you'll be my good luck charm," I said. She smiled shyly.

"How's that cow of yours?" she asked.

"She's healing nicely. My grandfather was very thankful. I really appreciated your help with that. I'm not sure if she would have recovered so gracefully if it weren't for you."

"I'm glad she's doing well." Angie looked down at the ground and then up at me with her big brown eyes. Her hair was tied loosely and pulled back off her pretty face.

"Are you here with any friends?" I asked.

"No, I took a ride down here alone, hoping I was going to bump into you."

A warm comfortable feeling filled my chest as I felt the heat rise into my face. "Well, would you like to accompany me to a fine party, down by the river? Some friends of mine, most of my teammates will be there." I held out my hand and assisted Angie while she walked around a family with small children having a picnic dinner. Angie kept her hand in mine as we walked together, toward my grandfather's truck.

"I need to be home early. I promised my father."

With my hand on her back, I helped Angie climb into my truck, shutting the door firmly behind her. I jumped into the driver's seat and looked at Angie sitting next to me.

"I promise you, I'll get you home early," I said as I put the truck into drive.

I took the long road on our journey to the river. The night started to get a little chilly and Pop's old pickup lacked a heating system. "Are you cold?" I asked Angie as I removed my jacket to give to her.

"Thank you, Jack." She put it on.

I watched her put my jacket on with amusement. "Sorry, I suppose it's a little big."

Angie started to laugh as she stretched out her arms. Her hands didn't quite fill the sleeves of my jacket. "At least it's warm and it smells nice." I secretly thanked Susie Mae for all her laundering skills. Angie slid a little closer to me on the bench seat and put her arm through mine. "Now, you'll be cold," she said, concerned.

"I can handle it, Ang. Don't worry about me."

We drove quietly up a few hills and then down a winding dirt road. It was silent but not in an awkward way. I could feel Angie's breast on my arm as she leaned into me. I could smell her perfume and the scent of her hair.

Angie broke the silence first. "Your Pop. He's a good man, Jack. When I was young and after my mother died, he helped my father many, many times. He and Susie would send food over and oftentimes, my father would drop me off with Susie to get some work done. My father speaks very highly of your grandfather."

A deep shot of pain went through my heart. I had heard that Angie's mother had died when she was very young. The horse she was riding had been spooked by a black bear. The mare took off suddenly and Angie's mother had fallen and hit her head. When they found her, it was too late. She had already lost significant blood and they couldn't save her. Her father was devastated.

"I'm sorry about your mother, Angie. Pop is a great man. I feel very fortunate to live here, in Indiana with him. I feel very close to him, like this is where I belong."

Angie looked at me and nodded her head quietly, agreeing with me. "I don't remember my mother. I know that I could never leave my father, though. I mean everything to him. He's sacrificed so much for me. How do you repay that? I feel so guilty sometimes. I wish he remarried, maybe started another family. He would never think of it. He only wanted to care for me."

I listened while Angie continued to talk about going to vet school and what it would mean to leave her father. I understood her confusion and her feelings of being torn. I listened as she spoke of feelings of guilt and sacrifice. I was glad she was talking, sharing her feelings. It felt good to connect to someone. Angie felt the same sort of commitment and loyalty to her family as I did to Pop and Susie.

"I've talked enough about me, Jack. What about you? Tell me about your family."

I pulled up along the river and parked my truck on the edge of the riverbank. I could see cars and classmates just a little ways up beyond the bend. "We'll have to walk from here. I don't want to get stuck in front of parked cars. I want to get you out of here on time to bring you home."

"That's fine. I don't mind walking." We sat in my truck a few minutes longer. We were in no big hurry to attend the party. Angie turned in her seat and faced me. She put her hand on my arm and rubbed the inside from my bicep to my elbow. "Tell me, Jack, about yourself. I don't know anything about you other than you moved here from Connecticut a few years back to live with your grandfather. Do you have other family?"

My heart felt heavy. I looked at Angie. She was so beautiful, so sweet and kind. Every inch of me wanted to confide in her about my mother and my brother. I hesitated. It was an awful, depressing story. The loss of my family was still raw, still deep. It wasn't what I wanted to talk about. It was too much, too soon.

"I came here from Connecticut and my grandfather saved my life."

Angie sat so close to me, my heart was racing. All these emotions we were sharing, it was very intense.

"I know how you feel about your father, Angie. I feel the same way about Pop. I would do anything and everything for him."

Angie reached up her hand and moved my hair off my forehead. She looked at me, patiently waiting for me to continue. I needed to change the subject.

I stared at her. I felt very close to her. I wanted to touch her, hold her, feel her body next to mine. I reached out and touched her face. I placed my hand behind her head and I pulled her close to me. Our faces almost touching, I lingered in front of her lips for a few seconds, and then I kissed her. Softly and slowly at first, I pulled her body into mine and I could feel the heat coming from our chests through our necks. I cupped her breast as our kiss became more passionate. She was incredibly sexy. Incredibly irresistible.

Just then, a banging on my door window.

"HEY, YOU TWO! ARE YOU COMING, OR WHAT?"

Angie and I jumped away from each other. Scared at first and then irritated at the intruder who just interrupted our special moment. I rolled down my window and it was Lionel, holding two bottles of beers. He handed the beers over to me with a wicked smile. "Sorry," he said quietly as he elbowed my arm. "Hey, Angie. Glad you could make it!"

"Hey Lionel. Thanks for the beer," Angie said smartly.

"Well, I'll let you two be," Lionel said as he started to walk away from the truck.

I looked over at Angie as she tried to adjust her shirt and fix her hair. "I guess we better head over to the party," I said. Angie smiled at me, playfully. She took her beer and clanked it on mine.

"Cheers!" she said happily. "Let's go have some fun!"

I opened my door and walked around my truck to open Angie's door. She hopped down into my arms and I held her briefly for a few seconds. I kissed her softly one last time and then we walked hand-in-hand to the party.

I smiled. I couldn't stop smiling.

CHAPTER 43

Lucy

We crossed the state line of Indiana. I had a constant lump in my throat. My heart palpitated and my thoughts were confused and ragged. There's so much to think about. I had so many feelings and fears. I constantly felt the need to rub Charles' shoulder as he sat in the front seat. My sister Kathryn teased me.

"Geez, Lucy, you're going to rub a hole in him."

"Sorry, Charles," I said. "I just can't imagine how you're feeling right now. I feel like a mess, but I'm sure you must feel ten times as bad."

"I feel okay, Lucy. I just hope we find my brother. If and when we find him, I am going to feel nothing but joy, excitement, and relief."

I nodded my head. "I'm afraid of what he'll say or feel or think. What if he doesn't care to see me, or us? What if he's angry?" I asked.

Charles turned around in his seat. "He's going to be fine, Lucy. Don't worry about that stuff. Whatever happens will happen."

"Yeah, I guess so." I sat back in my seat and watched as we drove by the cornfields, lots and lots of cornfields. I had never seen so much corn in my life.

"Take a right up there, Tommy. Pull into that feed store and I'll get out and ask the storeowner some questions. Maybe he knows my grandfather."

Tommy pulled into the parking lot and Charles got out of the vehicle. I turned to Amelia.

"Can you fix me a little, Amelia? How do I look?"

"Oh, Lucy. You're adorable. I mean, you've been traveling for two days, you haven't showered, and the only mirror you've seen is from a disgusting gas station bathroom. Still, you look amazing."

I slumped back into my chair. I flipped my hair back and layered it in a messy bun on top of my head. I thought to myself, *Maybe Jack's eyes aren't as blue as I remember them. Maybe his dimples aren't as cute.*

Charles jumped back into the car full of energy and excitement. *"They're here!"* he said, practically out of breath. "They're here! My grandfather's farm is up the road, five miles on the right. Jack plays football. There's a big game today at 1:00. They say he's the star quarterback!"

I sat up in my seat, ready to vomit at any moment. I never imagined feeling this nervous over reuniting with Jack. I'd thought of him for so long, and here we were, in the same town again.

"What time is it?" I asked as I looked for a watch in my purse.

"It's almost 2:00. We better get a move on. The football field is at the high school. The feed store owner said we couldn't miss it. Drive through town and take a left at the town hall." Charles' voice was breathy.

"Are you sure we should go right to the game?" I asked, trying to stall the encounter, buying some time. "Maybe we should go to the farm first and wait for Jack to return."

Charles turned around and looked at me. *"No way,* Lucy! I'm going. You could come or stay in the car. I don't care."

I sighed as Amelia started to rub my back. "Lucy, don't be so nervous."

I looked at my best friend. She was so sweet. She always understood how I was feeling. "I'm trying, Amelia. I can't help it."

"I'll be with you the entire time and if it's too awkward, I'll sit in the car with you. Okay?"

I smiled at Amelia. "Thank you, Amelia."

Amelia gave me a hug and a kiss on my cheek. "Let's go see Jack!"

Tommy drove through town and we saw the big banners on the green. "This must be an important game," he murmured.

"I can't believe my brother's a star quarterback. I feel proud, man."

Tommy slapped Charles on the back. "It's good to hear he's doing so well, Charles." Tommy pulled into the high school parking lot.

"There's no parking," Kathryn observed.

"Maybe try around back," Amelia suggested. We pulled around back and the football game came into view. Bleachers on all sides surrounded the massive field. The concession stand was busy with people and you could smell a barbecue.

"Yes!" Tommy stated.

"What?" I asked.

"There's food and I'm starving. Come on, Amelia. Let's get some grub."

"I'm too nervous to eat," I stated.

"What should we do, Charles?" Kathryn asked.

"Let's head down to the field and try to find a seat. It looks pretty crowded. We may have to stand."

We made our way to the field. I followed Charles and Kathryn.

"Can you tell what team he's on?" I asked. We stood at the fence and looked over the entire field. Both teams were wearing blue.

"Well, it looks like the visiting team is winning by four. I would guess that we're the team carrying the ball. Yes, see that? That coach has *DANVILLE* on the back of his shirt. That's Jack's team." I listened carefully as Charles explained the game of football. "The quarterback throws the ball, Lucy. You see, in the next play, Jack should have the ball first and then he will throw it to his teammate." I moved my head yes, like I understood what was happening. I'm not sure that it mattered, but it made Charles happy.

"Here he comes!" Charles yelled. "Number 4! You see him?"

"I do, I see him!" Oh my god, I couldn't believe that I was this close to him. He was just beyond the fence; a quick hop over and I could be with him, within seconds. Jack had his helmet on and he looked like every other player standing on the field, but I trusted Charles. If he said it was Jack, I had no reason to argue. I wanted to see his face; I needed to see his eyes.

Amelia and Tommy joined us, my brother eating a hamburger and a hotdog. Charles pointed out Jack to them.

"Close game. This is exciting," Tommy stated as he shoved food into his mouth. Amelia wrapped her arm around mine.

"How are you holding up?"

"Better," I said with a semi-convincing smile.

The crowd was going wild. It was the fourth quarter and there was less than two minutes on the clock. "Boy, we made it here just in the nick of time," I stated to no one in particular.

"Sure did." Charles was listening.

Jack made another attempt at a throw. It was a beautiful throw, but the receiver dropped it.

"Shit!" Charles said under his breath.

My nervousness had been replaced by my anxiety for Jack's team and my desire for him to make the winning touchdown. You could feel the entire crowd was counting on him; so much pressure. Amelia and Kathryn had begun a cheering squad to the right of me. You couldn't help but feel the energy from the crowd. All eyes were on the game.

The team set up for the last attempt at ten yards. "They're either going to try to run the ball or Jack's going to make one last pass," Charles explained.

I watched Jack as he huddled his teammates. My eyes couldn't leave him. I watched his every move. He was so strong, so graceful. *Please, Dear Lord. Give him what he wants.* The teams lined up, Jack stepped back with the ball, and he looked and looked and then he passed. *Please, please, please.*

"HE CAUGHT IT!" I yelled and screamed and clapped.

"RUN, RUN, RUN!" Charles was yelling. Jack stood watching his teammate run the ball to the goal line.

"Wow, he's fast!" Tommy stated. We held our breath as the running back crossed the goal line.

"YEAH!" I yelled with my arms up in the air. Jack jumped up and you could see the excitement of the entire team. "They won!" I yelled. "They won!"

Charles was beaming with pride and exhilaration. They high-fived each other. "Yeah!"

The fans started to empty out onto the football field. We lost track of Jack. The crowd was too big and the celebration was fierce. It was clear Charles wanted to run out on the field, but I don't think he wanted to disrupt Jack's moment of fame.

"Let's just hang back here for awhile. We'll let the crowd die down and then we'll try to find him. Maybe after he gets out of the locker room," Charles said. Everyone agreed.

"We can probably find a seat now," I mentioned, laughing. We walked onto the bleachers and sat for a while. "Your grandfather must be here," I said to Charles.

Charles scanned the area around him. "I don't know what he looks like."

I turned around and looked at the parking lot behind us. The cars formed a procession line and every vehicle was beeping their horn in unison. I looked around at all the happy people. What a great day for them. I watched the building where the locker rooms and restrooms were. I could see some of the football players starting to emerge. There were several classmates hanging around, as well as parents and grandparents.

"Maybe we should head down to that area, Charles." I pointed to the small crowd assembled by the building.

"Yeah, let's do that."

My stomach started to do somersaults. We walked over to the standing crowd and watched the people around us. I watched the door as the players continued to exit the building. *Be cool, Lucy. Don't be too obvious. Don't fall apart the first moment you see him, and definitely DON'T CRY!* I closed my eyes and prayed for the strength I needed to keep my emotions in tact. It had been so long and so many years had passed. He was important to me, but I was scared. What if I didn't matter to him? What if he was casual and unmoved?

The door opened. It was Jack! His hair was wet from the shower and he was wearing ragged jeans and a white T-shirt. He had a helmet in one hand and a cowboy hat in the other. He placed his cowboy hat on his head. He smiled, a beautiful smile with big deep dimples. His eyes sparkled blue. He'd grown into a man. His arms were strong and built and his chest was solid as a rock. I stood there in terror. I couldn't move or speak. God, he was handsome.

An elderly man and woman approached him first. This must be his grandfather. I looked over at Charles. He was waiting to make his existence known. Jack's grandfather hugged him affectionately, his eyes bursting with pride and respect. Jack picked the woman up and kissed her on the cheek. I smiled at the show of affection he had for his grandparents.

Then the girl. Where did she come from? Why is she kissing him? *A very attractive girl.* She was hugging him tightly. *I might die. I just might die.* I wanted to run. Amelia was immediately at my side. My heart was pounding in my ears. *Oh god. Why am I here?* I stared at them. They looked so happy. He was laughing and talking. I couldn't take my eyes off him. He was beautiful. He was everything I imagined.

He's got his arm around the girl and they were walking straight for us. *He hasn't recognized us yet. He doesn't know we are here.*

Charles stepped forward first. He stood there in the crowd as we slowly backed away from him, giving him space. Jack looked at him quickly and then looked away. Then he stopped and stared. My heart was pounding. Jack removed his arm from the girl and stepped forward in disbelief.

"Charles?" he said, his mouth open, his face full of shock. The crowd seemed to stop and gaze as silence fell upon us, all else falling away as the boys stared into each other's faces, one not believing the other's appearance, Jack blinking his eyes several times as he focused on his brother, seemingly convincing himself that it wasn't a dream. That he was real.

Charles nodded his head yes and the boys collided into each other. They tried to out-strength each other in a series of hugs and lifts and wrestling moves, laughing, hugging, and kissing each other's faces. Both talking animatedly: "I can't believe it! Look at you! All grown up!"

"How did you get here?" Jack asked, holding on to his brother. "Pop! Pop! Come here. You won't believe it! It's Charles!"

Bystanders stood stationary as they witnessed the unfolding event. One gentleman stopped his wife to whisper in her ear while pointing at Charles and Jack as the smiles of others spread across their faces as they stopped to observe.

The girl stepped aside. Charles' grandfather approached him swiftly and eagerly. He too was standing back, watching the event unfold. He took Charles' hand and shook it and pulled him into a manly hug. He grabbed both boys on either side of him and pulled them in, like a grandfather sandwich. I looked around at the crowd. Everyone was smiling. One man started to clap and cheer, encouraging the ongoing excitement of the obvious reunion and the winning of the game. Others joined in.

Jack's grandfather was talking with Charles, inviting him to the farm. "You're staying for some time, I hope."

I watched Jack. I felt so happy for him. Amelia was squeezing my hand. *I think she's more nervous now than I am.* Jack started to look around him. He saw Kat and Tommy first. He nodded his head at them and smiled, "I can't believe you guys are here!"

He looked at Amelia and I. Our eyes locked. My heart stopped. I couldn't move or breathe. Jack stood still, just the same. "Oh my god," he said softly. "Lucy!"

I started to smile, but my eyes watered. *Oh god, please don't cry.* Jack's face looked somewhat concerned. He stepped toward me and I to him. I quickly wiped my eyes with the back of my hand and tried to give him a strong, encouraging smile. He instinctively reached out for me.

I gathered myself, stepped forward, and jumped up into his arms. I fit him, perfectly. He held me and carried me and squeezed me tight. I let my emotions take over and I cried quietly into his shoulder. I couldn't help it. These past two days had been full of so much emotion, worry, and anxiety for me. *He remembers. He remembers me.* Relief flooded my body and the anxiety fled my soul.

"Lucy," he said quietly while he held my head into him. "I can't believe it."

We stayed like this for a long moment. Jack slowly put me down on my feet. He looked at me, he looked at Charles, he looked at Kat and Tommy…and then he smiled.

That beautiful, dreamy, country boy smile.

CHAPTER 44

Julia

Julia waited for her father to come home from the hospital. It was late, way past ten at night. She hadn't heard from him all day. She sat in the kitchen and drank a cup of decaffeinated tea. She was so tired but she wanted to hear that her mother was going to be alright.

The words that her father was saying didn't seem real. "She's got pneumonia, Julia. She wasn't eating properly at your grandmother's. She's lost so much weight. She's very weak." Her father looked exhausted. "They have her on oxygen and they've sedated her to keep her calm. She's confused and disoriented. They say she may be experiencing a mental breakdown. They're giving her high doses of antibiotic to help fight the pneumonia."

Julia stood and stared at her father. She had no words of comfort for him. No words of wisdom or promising words of hope.

Her father stood and made his way for the stairs. "I need to go to bed, Julia. Tomorrow, we need to find your brother and sister. They need to come home."

She nodded her head yes, and watched her father as he disappeared into his room. How was she going to reach Lucy and Tommy? She would think about it tomorrow, she guessed. It had been a long day. She needed to go to bed and worry about it after she had gotten some rest.

Pneumonia. What the fuck?

CHAPTER 45

Jack

I watched Tommy in my rearview mirror as he followed me, maneuvering his car through town on the way to Pop's farm. I uncomfortably glanced over at Angie, her once attentive and supportive attitude toward me now changed. I invited her to join us at my grandfather's, but she delicately declined the invitation and insisted that she needed to go home. I had hoped that my feelings for Lucy weren't so obvious, but I think that they were. It was never my intentions to hurt Angie's feelings. I rested my forehead on the window and felt the cool sensation of the glass on my face. I slowly exited the car and let Angie out of the vehicle, stopping her briefly before she ran for her front door. "I'm sorry, Angie; this was unexpected."

She turned to me and smiled carefully. "I'm happy for you, Jack. Enjoy your family and please don't worry about me."

She stepped eagerly around me and made her way to the small farmhouse that she shared with her father.

I felt sorry for Angie and for the awkward encounter, but I also felt relief that she was gone. I couldn't help the feelings that I had for Lucy. They were so intense; we shared so much history together. She was a huge part of my routine here. Every day I read her note; every day I thought about her. And to have my brother back; I just wanted to stare at him. I kept waiting for someone to pinch me or jump back out behind the curtain and say, "Sorry, Jack…we were just kidding." But it was real. They were here for me. They came for me and they found me and I couldn't be more grateful.

I jumped back into my truck and looked over at my brother. He was waiting for me, waiting for his chance to speak and to be heard.

"Jack, I missed you so much. There was never a day that went by that I didn't think about you or wonder what ever became of you. I could never forgive myself for what I did to you, leaving you like that when we were young. I'm sorry, Jack. I'm so sorry."

I looked over at my brother, tears in my eyes and forgiveness in my heart. I hoped that Charles could see my understanding in my expression. All I wanted was to move forward with my brother in my life. I vowed never to let anything come between us again. This was a second chance on having a real family, and I didn't want to blow it.

"Charles, it's alright. I had a good life here with Pop. I'm just sorry you missed it. What's important is that you are here now and I want to spend as much time with you as we can. We can forget all that happened before and be brothers again. I can't believe you're here!" I leaned over and punched my brother in his arm then grabbed him and put my arm around him while I drove, carelessly swerving past the cornfields. I drove up the hill, through the meadow, around the corner and then up the dirt road. As I pulled into the driveway of our little farmhouse, I couldn't help but feel whole and proud of my life and in the home that was provided for me. I couldn't wait to share the farm with my brother and my friends. I recognized that familiar feeling that this was home now, especially since everyone that I loved so dear was here with me. I felt so honored and blessed. Charles and I hopped out of my vehicle first and we were quickly at each other's side, arms around each other.

I stared at my brother once again, feeling complete for the first time in a long time. That missing piece that had haunted me, put back into its place. My heart was full of love and gratitude for my family. Pure joy and happiness filled my soul as I watched Tommy pull up his vehicle along the side of mine. I could see Lucy's eyes through the window. Her smile—

she made my heart miss a beat, the way she looked at me. I would never be this happy again, in this moment.

This was my life, this was my dream life.

CHAPTER 46

Lucy

I exited Tommy's vehicle and stood and glanced at my surroundings. The farm was so organized. The gardens and plants were beautiful, the barn neat and orderly. No clutter, no disarray. Jack walked toward me with a prideful smile. "Impressive, right?"

"It's beautiful, Jack," I replied.

"After you get settled, I'll take you on a small tour. Do you have your things? I can show you and the girls to your room and you can use the bathrooms if you need to. I know you've traveled quite a distance."

"YES!" Amelia hollered. "I would *love* a shower!"

Jack looked at Amelia and smiled. "I don't believe we've met."

"Oh, Jack, I'm sorry. This is my best friend, Amelia Rose."

Amelia beamed her charming smile toward Jack. "It's a pleasure. I'm so happy to meet the person I've heard so many things about. You have a very devoted brother there"—Amelia nodded toward Charles—"and a very devoted friend over here." Amelia nodded toward me.

"Yes, I see this," Jack said with a sly smile. He looked at me, eyes locking, no words spoken.

"Back to that shower, Jack," Amelia prompted.

"Oh, yes. Follow me, ladies."

Charles walked over to Kathryn and helped her with her bag. "How are you feeling, Charles?" Kat asked in a whisper.

"This is unbelievable, Kat. I feel like I want to jump, scream, and rejoice to the heavens." Charles grabbed Kat's face and gave her a big kiss on her lips. "I feel *awesome!*"

Kat laughed out loud. The two held hands and walked toward the farmhouse. Susie Mae opened the screen door and waved everyone to come join her.

"I've got drinks, snacks, and clean towels," Susie stated as she ushered everyone into the kitchen.

Pop walked into the room carrying some old newspapers. He handed them to Jack. "Carry these to the fire pit. We're going to have ourselves a good old-fashioned campfire barbecue."

"Okay, Pop. Come on, boys. I'll show you my room after and you could settle in." Jack and the boys walked out of the house toward the fire pit. Pop walked through the kitchen and stood at the screen door watching Jack and Charles start a fire.

"Susie Mae? Can you believe it? Both my boys here, together," Pop said, grinning ear to ear. Susie stopped and rubbed Pop's back affectionately.

"It's a great day to celebrate," she said. "Come with me, ladies. I'm sure you're dying to settle in."

"Thank you so much, Susie. Pop? Should we call you Pop?" I asked Jack's grandfather. Pop stopped and placed his arm around my shoulder.

"I owe you young folks a great deal of gratitude and appreciation. You've brought these two boys together and have reunited my family. You're all very special to me. Yes, please, call me Pop."

We followed Susie Mae up the stairs and into the spare bedroom at the back of the house. "You girls can use the bathroom down the hall on the left. You babies look tired.

Here are some towels for you. Take your time, clean up, and I'll make a nice dinner. Can I get you anything else?" she asked kindly. Susie Mae reminded me of a younger version of my great grandmother. Short, round, and plump with bright eyes.

"No, thank you very much. You've been very gracious," I responded.

"Yes, thank you," Kat and Amelia added.

"Alright then, I'll see you shortly. Call me if you need me." Susie Mae turned and left and I collapsed on the bed, completely exhausted.

Amelia quickly pulled me up into a sitting position. "*Lucy!* Oh my god! Jack is so handsome."

I fell back onto the bed and put my hands over my face. "He's got a girlfriend," I said sadly.

Amelia grabbed a towel while I sat on the bed, pouting. "She might have been his girlfriend, but he can't take his eyes off of you." Amelia headed for the bathroom and stopped at the doorway and stared at me. "Lucy, we're here. We found Jack. Be happy!"

I thought about her comment for a split second. *She's right.* I needed to get it together. Amelia disappeared into the bathroom to clean up while Kathryn found a cozy home in a

Queen Anne chair. As she put her feet up, she commented, "What a comfortable room."

I looked around the room. The four-poster bed was as soft as the clouds in the sky. Beautiful antique furniture filled the space. The floors were wide board with old, braided rugs scattered about. "This reminds me of Great Grandma's house up in Vermont."

Kat nodded. "At some point, we need to call home."

"Why don't we wait until morning? I'm sure Pop will let us use his phone."

"Yeah, okay."

"Do you want to use the shower next?" I asked.

"Sure, if Amelia doesn't take her sweet time."

I laughed and snuggled up on a pillow and closed my eyes. "Just wake me when it's my turn," I said. I didn't hear Kathryn's response. I felt my body relax and my mind go blank.

When I woke, the room was dark and there was a quilt laid upon me. "Oh my god," I said as I jumped up. I could hear faint voices and laughter coming from outside. I went to the window but I couldn't see anyone. I looked at myself quickly in the mirror. *I should probably shower,* I thought to myself. *I'm going to kill Kathryn. Why didn't she wake me?*

I took a quick shower and changed. I felt rested. I ran down the stairs and into the kitchen. Susie Mae was at the kitchen sink cleaning some dishes.

"There you are," she said to me.

"I'm sorry. I hope I didn't miss anything. I guess I fell asleep," I said, embarrassed.

"Oh, sit down, dear. Let me make you a plate. You haven't missed anything but dinner."

Susie placed a generous plate of fried chicken, potato salad, and corn in front of me and rubbed my head like a child. I smiled at her affection.

"This looks fantastic, Susie. Thank you. I'm starving," I said.

"Of course you are. You're too thin. You need to eat, Lucy."

I laughed. "You sound like my mother."

Susie turned around and faced me while she continued drying a dish. "Tell me, how is it you kids came across Charles and made your way here, to Indiana?" she asked.

I stared up at her, not sure how much Jack had shared with her and not sure what I should say. "Charles and Jack were my neighbors growing up. They lived down the street from me," I answered. Susie looked at me, urging me to continue. I took a bite of my food and thought about what more I should share. "I was with Jack the day they found his mother."

Susie stopped drying her dish. She stood in front of the table and pulled out a chair and sat close to me. "That day was very difficult for Jack," Susie said. "He had nightmares for a long time."

I nodded. I understood what she was saying. "It was difficult for me too because Jack was gone the next day. I never got to say goodbye. I've thought about him ever since."

Susie placed her hand on top of mine. "Those boys have been through some heartache."

"Yes, they have. When Charles came back to town looking for Jack, we decided it was time to try to find him. We were very lucky. We had to drive far but we didn't have to look far for him," I said with a chuckle. "He seems so happy. I'm so glad he has you and Pop. His mother...well, she was different," I said as I finished my plate of food. I stood and placed my plate into the sink. "Let me help you clean up."

"Nonsense. I want you to go sit by the fire, enjoy your friends. They are all waiting for you."

I turned and walked toward the screen door. I could see the fire pit and everyone sitting around it. Jack had his back to me. I could hear Amelia animatedly telling the story about how we were a part of the KKK demonstration yesterday in Pennsylvania. I turned to Susie and thanked her for a wonderful meal. Susie turned and gave me a motherly hug.

"You're welcome, sweetheart. Now go!"

I opened the screen door and walked over to the fire pit.

"Lucy!" Amelia stood to meet me halfway. "We didn't want to wake you. You looked so tired."

Jack also stood. "Come, sit!" he said as he offered me his chair. I smiled at him.

"I don't know what happened," I said, embarrassed.

Pop started to laugh. "It's that bed upstairs. It will suck you in and next thing you know, you're sound asleep."

"It really is a nice bed, so soft," I said with a smile.

"We were just listening to Amelia fill us in on your road trip adventures," Jack said to me in a semi-whisper.

"Yes, well, Amelia can be a little dramatic, if you know what I mean."

"Not true," Amelia stated in her pouty voice.

Tommy grabbed Amelia's chair and pulled her closer to him. "I love your stories, Amelia," he said affectionately. She gave him a quick kiss on his lips and snuggled into his arms.

"Thank you, Tommy."

Pop stood to stretch his legs. "Well kids, as much as I would love to sit here all night, I think I'll go in and help Susie Mae clean up and then head to bed."

Charles stood and gave his grandfather a hug. "Thank you, sir. Do you need help, Pop?"

Pop beamed at Charles. "No, son, I can manage. We'll talk again in the morning." Pop tipped his hat and said, "Night, y'all."

"Good night, Pop," we responded. We all sat quietly until Pop was safely out of earshot and into the house.

Jack leaned over and whispered in my ear. "Do you want to go for a walk? I'd love to show you around and to talk to you privately."

My heart nearly skipped a beat. I could feel my hands sweaty with perspiration. "Yeah, sure. I'd love that." I stood and followed Jack around the set of chairs situated near the fire pit.

"Where are you two going?" Amelia asked.

"We'll be back," Jack said quickly. He grabbed my hand and led me down the yard until we reached the horse barn. He opened the barn door and allowed me to enter first. I walked past the first stall. I could hear my boots clapping on the barn wood floor. The smell of the hay mixed with horse manure was almost intoxicating. Jack shut the door behind us. "It's starting to get chilly. Are you warm, Lucy?"

I looked at him shyly and smiled, "Yes, I'm fine, Jack."

As I approached the second horse stall, a mare poked her head out. "Who's this beauty?" I asked as I pet her face gently, hoping not to startle her.

"Oh, that's Ginger Girl. She's my baby." Jack joined me and rubbed Ginger's head roughly. "Ginger, this is my friend Lucy." Ginger threw her head back as if to say, *I don't really care.*

I started to laugh. "I don't think she likes sharing you, Jack."

"Oh, she'll get used to the idea. She'll learn to love you." He stared at me and that familiar knowing silence lingered in the air.

My heart rate was racing. *Relax, Lucy.*

"Well, she's beautiful," I said to break the silence. I stared at Ginger and then looked back at Jack.

"You look beautiful, Lucy," Jack stated. I met Jack's stare while my heart was burning from anticipation. Jack took my hand delicately. "Lucy, Charles told me it was you who insisted on finding me. It was you who pressured everyone to act. I've never forgotten that day, Luce. It's obvious you haven't either."

I watched Jack's eyes. They never waver. I'm not sure how to respond. I'm afraid if I speak, I will cry. I'm afraid if I speak, I will tell him how much he means to me, how sorry I am, and how I've longed for him.

I said nothing. I held his hand tightly, not wanting to let go.

Jack reached into his pocket and pulled out a note. He handed it to me. I opened it. I couldn't believe my eyes. It was my handwriting—my letter to Jack, the day he disappeared. *He has it. He's kept it all this time.* I shook my head no, in disbelief.

"Lucy, look at me."

I looked up at Jack, my eyes full of tears.

"I know that day was difficult for you, I saw it in your face. I felt so guilty for having involved you. I'm sorry I didn't get to say goodbye. I've thought about that day, every day since. I've thought of you and I've read this note every day, since the day I received it. It was the only thing that brought me peace. The only thing I had that was you."

Jack put his hands around my waist and pulled me closer to him. "I just want to thank you. I want to tell you I've had a good life." Jack looked into my eyes like he did so many years before. His voice so sincere, his eyes sparkling blue, his beautiful smile. There was nothing I could say. He'd said it all. All I could do was give myself to him. All I wanted was to feel him and to hold him.

"Jack—" I said, hesitantly.

He bent down into my face, his lips so close to mine, our noses practically touching. I could feel his heart beating just as loud as mine. He grabbed my face gently, he tilted my head toward his, and he kissed me. My tears couldn't help but escape my eyes, my hands grabbed tightly onto his biceps. He kissed me, soft and gentle at first and then fierce and desperate. We held each other and kissed passionately, each of us not getting enough of the other, each of us trying to drain our souls of the lost time, the pain, and the heartache.

My mind was spinning. I could hardly believe what was happening. I could feel the excitement and thrill of Jack touching me and kissing me throughout my entire body. Jack stopped and softly started to kiss my cheeks, my eyes, and my forehead. He whispered to me, "Thank you, Lucy. You have no idea how important you are to me."

I'm in heaven. The years of build-up, worry, thoughts, and questions all colliding together into one kiss. I would never experience a greater moment. I didn't want it to end.

Ginger Girl began to rear her head and kick her feet. Jack paused for a moment and looked into my eyes. "I'm sensing she's jealous of you," he said with one last kiss. Jack pulled away from me and walked over to Ginger. "Calm down, girl. Calm down." He rubbed her mane. I watched him as he lovingly soothed his horse and nearly put her to sleep with his soft voice. I smiled at his attentiveness, his composure, and his concern for Ginger. "I'll be back tomorrow, girl. We'll go for a run," he said quietly to Ginger. Jack turned and approached me. "Perhaps we should head back. I'm sure you're still tired, Lucy. We'll have more time tomorrow to catch up."

I wanted to scream, *No! Not yet*, but I nodded my head yes. I was completely disappointed. I didn't want more time away. I would have preferred to stay the night with Jack. I would have preferred to lie in his arms and sleep like a baby.

We went back. As we approached the campfire, we noticed everyone has left and gone to bed.

"Looks like we're the last ones standing," Jack said in good humor. He put his arm around my waist and we continued to walk toward the farmhouse and into the kitchen. "You're quiet, Lucy. What are you thinking? Are you okay?"

I smiled and looked at my old friend from the past. "It's just overwhelming, Jack, to be with you again. I have so many feelings. Strong feelings. I'm not sure what to do with them."

Jack stopped me in the middle of the kitchen. The lights were dim. "It's overwhelming for me too, Lucy. I need to tell you something." Jack wrapped his strong arms around me. He pulled me into him one last time. "I'm never going to lose you again. You're very special to me, Lucy. I just want you to know that. You'll always be a part of me, no matter what." Jack spoke softly, trying not to wake anyone in the house. He spoke dream words. Words a girl like me only wished she could ever hear from a boy like Jack. I closed my eyes and waited for it. I waited for his touch.

Jack bent down to kiss me again. He briefly touched my lips with his and he whispered, "It's not over for us, Lucy. It's just beginning." He continued to kiss me softly and then he picked me up and hugged me, like he may never let me go. I wrapped my arms around his neck and held him tight.

My mind was screaming with joy. *I love him. I love him. I love him.* It was all I could think.

Jack gently put me down again, and kissed me one last time. "Goodnight, Lucy. Sweet dreams."

I wanted to say, *I love you Jack. I love you*, but the only words that escaped me were "I'll see you in the morning." Jack turned and headed toward his bedroom as I walked up the stairs quietly and into my room. I smiled to myself as I lay on the bed. *I love him.*

The next morning, I woke to Kathryn shaking me on my bed. "Lucy, wake up! Get your things together," she said hurriedly. I opened my eyes and jumped up, startled.

"What's wrong, Kat? Why are you packing?" I asked, my voice full of concern.

"It's Mom! I just spoke with Julia. She's sick, Lucy, real sick. We need to leave now. Julia's been looking for us for days."

I closed my eyes and said a quick prayer. Why did we come here? I should have never left. Something bad was happening. I quickly got dressed and followed Kathryn down into the kitchen where Amelia and Tommy were waiting for us. Tommy took our bags and went outside toward the car. I looked around at everyone's faces. Everyone looked concerned. No one was speaking. My eyes met Jack's.

"Jack," I said as I stepped toward him. "I need to go."

"I know, Lucy. It's important. It's your mother."

I turned to Susie Mae and Pop. "Thank you all very much for your kindness."

Susie Mae stepped toward me and gave me a quick hug. "You stay in touch, now. Keep us posted."

"Yes, ma'am," I responded. I turned and opened the screen door and headed toward the car. Kat was saying goodbye to Charles.

I heard Charles saying, "I'm going to stay here with Jack and Pop to catch up."

Kat looked disappointed but she kissed him goodbye. She hugged him and said, "I'll see you soon."

Jack held the door open for me as I settled into the seat next to Kathryn. He shut the door and I rolled down the window. I leaned up against the door and said, "Jack, I'm sorry. This is unexpected. I wish we had more time."

Jack leaned into the window and kissed my lips. "Me too, Lucy. Stay in touch. Let me know how your mother is, please."

I kissed him again. "Goodbye, Jack."

"Bye, Lucy."

Thomas started the car and began to reverse out of the driveway. Pop, Susie Mae, Charles, and Jack waved goodbye as we left. I turned around in my seat and watched them as we drove down the road. I watched as the house got smaller and smaller and smaller. Tears filled my eyes. My heart was heavy.

He was gone, once again.

CHAPTER 47

Lucy

The trip home was long and torturous. Amelia tried her best to keep things light and simple. She made small talk and was overly eager to help us, console us, if we needed her. I just wanted to get home as fast as possible. We decided not to stop for the night. Thomas and Kathryn took turns driving. We drove straight through until we reached Connecticut, a thirteen-hour depressed journey of worry and concern.

I felt such relief when we crossed the Connecticut border. It had been after midnight by the time we reached our driveway. Julia was awake waiting for us to arrive. I jumped out of the car and ran up the three-stair porch that entered into our kitchen.

"Lucy!" Julia announced as I barged into the house. "Oh, I'm so glad you're finally home. Kat! Hey, Thomas! How was your trip?" Julia asked as she hugged us hello. Thomas

314

dropped his bag on the floor and walked past us to the hallway going toward his room.

"*Long*," he said in a grumpy voice. "I need to shower," he mumbled as he disappeared.

"How's Mom?" I asked, looking to Julia for answers.

"The doctors are doing the best they can for her. She's on oxygen, but she's not conscious. Dad's been at her side for three days now. He only stops to come home, eat, and shower and then he's back at the hospital."

"How did this happen?" I asked, my eyes tearing from the long, exhausting drive home and from the overwhelming concern for my mother. Kat walked over to me and rubbed my back gently. "I feel so guilty," I added. "I shouldn't have left. I should have stayed and helped you, Julia."

Julia held onto my hand as she spoke to me. "Lucy, there was nothing you could have done to stop this. Mom's not right in her mind. She stopped eating and her body is having a real difficult time healing itself. You had nothing to do with that."

"It just seems like this happened so fast."

"Can we see Mom?" Kat asked Julia.

"Why don't you girls get some sleep? I'll wake you early and we'll all go to the hospital together. It's too late now; they won't have visitors at this hour."

Kat and I both accepted Julia's advice and we all slowly retreated to our bedrooms.

I said goodnight to my sisters and I closed and stood behind my bedroom door. I walked over to my bed and as I felt my body fall onto the soft mattress, all I could think about was how happy I was to be home. How happy I was to be in my bed, in my room. I wished for nothing more than to talk to Jack. So much was happening in such a small amount of time. I closed my eyes and pictured Jack's face. The memory of him kissing me ran through my thoughts. My time with Jack seemed imagined. I thought about that moment, I thought about our trip, and then I thought about my poor mother, lying still in her hospital bed. All my thoughts, everything around me, all that was happening seemed so unreal.

I tried to will myself to sleep. I tried to clear my mind so I could rest my eyes. I slowly felt my body falling, falling into a dream state. I felt my worries and anxiety disappear into nothing. I was so thankful. So thankful for the reprieve from reality.

Goodnight, Mama. I'll be with you tomorrow.

CHAPTER 48

Lucy

I heard the ringing in my head. It wouldn't stop. *Ring. Ring. Ring.* I carefully opened my eyes, not wanting to see the sunlight beaming into my bedroom. It was the phone. It was ringing again. I slowly dragged my body out of my bed and I started to walk down the stairs. I could barely walk. My body was so stiff. Must have been from the long car drive, I thought to myself.

"Hello," I said as I picked up the receiver.

"Lucy?" my dad asked, surprised to hear me.

"Hey, Dad, yes, it's me."

"When did you get home?"

"We arrived around midnight last night. It was such a long drive and we were so tired. Julia thought we should try to get some rest and then we would come to see Mom this morning."

"Is Julia awake?" my dad asked. His voice sounded tired and defeated.

"I don't think so. Do you need me to wake her?"

My dad released a huge sigh on the other end of the phone. "Yes, honey. I want you all to get ready and come to the hospital. It's important."

"Is everything alright?" I asked in a wavering voice.

"No, honey, it's not. Get your sisters and come here quickly, okay?"

"Okay, Dad. We will."

"Thank you, sweetheart. I'll see you soon."

I hung up the phone and stood frozen in my slippers.

Julia walked down the stairs, groggy from sleep and from the early hour of the morning. I looked up at her, my face contorted with fear. "Dad wants us at the hospital, as soon as possible."

Julia put her face down and started to shake her head. She turned and walked back up the stairs. "You wake the kids," she called behind her. "I'll wake Kat and Thomas."

I managed to move my legs and do as Julia asked. I walked into Kaylan and Jessica's room. "Kaylan. We need to wake up. Jessica, wake up sleepy head." I opened their curtains to let some light into their bedroom.

"Lucy?" Kaylan responded, surprised. "What are you doing here? When did you get home?"

"We drove in last night, but it was late, I didn't want to wake you."

"We missed you!" Jessica declared.

"Mom's sick," Kaylan said.

"I know. I'm sorry I wasn't here to help her. Can you girls get ready quickly? Dad called and he wants us at the hospital." I watched the girls as they climbed out of their beds. Jessica started to cry.

"Mom's dying, isn't she?" she whimpered.

"Jessica, why would you say that? She's going to be fine," I said.

"You don't know, Lucy; you haven't seen her. She's not fine. She doesn't know who we are. She can't even talk."

I stared at the girls as they started to dress, the reality of my mother's condition starting to settle in. They couldn't possibly be right, my sisters. They must be confused as to my mother's real condition. Perhaps they heard the doctors wrong. Perhaps they were over-exaggerating. My hands started to shake as I walked back into my bedroom. I threw on my jeans and sneakers and pulled my hair up into a messy bun. I brushed my teeth quickly and then went to check on Mikey. Thomas had already alerted him and he was up and ready. I ran down the stairs where everyone was waiting for me. I looked at all the sad faces standing in the kitchen.

"It's going to be okay, guys. There's no way Mom's *not* going to make it," I said in my most positive, uplifting voice. Thomas grabbed his keys off the counter and led our family out of the house to the car.

The drive to the hospital took twenty minutes, the pit in my stomach growing larger and larger the closer and closer we came to the hospital. The car ride was quiet but heavy with worry and anticipation. Thomas parked our car and we made our way up the large concrete stairway leading from the parking lot to the hospital emergency room. Julia took the lead through the hospital corridors, to the appropriate elevators that led us to the critical care unit on the fifth floor. We entered the wide double doors to the reception area and I saw my father talking quietly to one of the nurses on the unit.

I walked quickly toward him and threw my arms around him. "Hi, honey," my father stated as he hugged me tightly. One by one, we greeted him.

320

"I want to speak to you kids, before you go in and see your mother. Come, sit down in the waiting room so I can talk with you." My father led us to the private waiting room to fill us in on our mother's condition. "The doctors have started to administer morphine," my father started.

"What's morphine?" Kaylan asked.

My father looked lovingly at Kaylan. "Morphine is a drug that they are giving Mom so that she feels no pain. So she won't suffer."

Kaylan stared at my father and pretended to understand what he was telling her.

"Your mother's pneumonia has gotten the best of her. She is no longer breathing on her own. The doctors use morphine to ease her suffering and to help her pass peacefully and painlessly."

Help her pass peacefully. I could hear my father's words but I still couldn't believe it. I couldn't get my head wrapped around it. My mother. My beautiful, wonderful mother. How could this be? My father continued to speak, but I could barely hear him. My head was spinning with thoughts of denial and objection.

"Her breathing is labored. It sounds like a low gurgling sound, like a crackling in her chest. You'll hear her take every breath until she takes her last one. I can't tell you when this will be. It could take ten minutes, it could take five hours."

I watched my father as he tried so hard to be strong. He was speaking so matter-of-factly. Mikey stood close to him and occasionally glanced up into his face with his big brown eyes. Everyone else appeared to be in shock. Eyes wide and faces full of raw emotion.

My father finally finished talking and led us into my mother's room. I walked in, so fearful of what I was going to see. Thomas went to her first. He knelt down beside my mother and grabbed her hand tight. Sobs of sorry escaped his body as he kissed her hand repeatedly. "You were a great mother; you were the best. I'm so sorry, Mama. I'm so sorry," he cried. I watched in shock as the emotions poured out of my brother's mouth.

I watched my mother as she lay in her bed. I remembered the fear that I felt as a young child, the fear that I may lose my mother. I would worry and cry at night at the thought of living my young life without her. My childish fears that seemed to surface now, the horrifying realization that the fear was real, not just a part of my imagination.

The tubes had been removed from her face and her body lay covered in layers of blankets. Jessica made her way next. She climbed into the bed right beside my mother as if they were lying together watching a movie. She snuggled in as best as she could and held her other hand, tight.

Julia looked at me next and gave her silent signal that I should go to her and say my final goodbyes. I went to my mother's bedside and kissed her face softly. Tears welled up into my eyes as I moved her hair off her face. I carefully pulled the covers up tightly around her neck. I felt the need to beg her. I wasn't going to let her off so easily.

"Please Mom, stay with us. Stay with us and be our mother. We need you. We love you, please." I kissed her again and again, crying and sobbing until my father had his hand on my shoulder. I moved and sat in the back of the room and watched my other siblings one by one say good-bye. They were painful, agonizing moments, watching my mother breathing and waiting for the moment when those breaths would stop.

My mother had lost so much weight. Her face was rose-colored but thin and pale. Her hair, dark from color, yet grey from the months of lack of care.

I watched as she took her last breath. I watched her chest rise and fall, my eyes glued onto her body as her lungs exhaled and relaxed for the last time. I listened for the guttural rattling in her chest to continue, but there was silence. I watched for the line on the machine to jump once again, but it didn't. I stared in disbelief at my lifeless mother.

I looked around at my family. Everyone's faces staring at her figure, everyone's faces not believing. Her face transformed from rose-colored and soft to grey-toned and stiff within seconds. I stared at her body lying there dead in the hospital room. As my mourning family left her bedside, I looked back at her. I felt nothing for the body that was left behind.

My mother was no longer there. She was gone.

We left the hospital that day in wordless despair. I felt absolute disbelief when I thought about my dead mother. My heart and soul was heavy with anguish. I could do nothing but lie in my bed and cry. I needed to get it together. I needed to help my family with the arrangements and help Julia with Kaylan and Jessica. I felt so much pain and guilt. I slept restlessly.

The night before my mother's funeral, I felt her. She had awoken me from a dead sleep. She ran her finger down my nose as if to say, *I see you, Lucy. I'm watching you. Mama's okay now.*

I shot up in my bed and looked around my darkened room. There was no one. There was nothing, but I felt her. I immediately felt peace in my heart.

I smiled to myself and spoke out loud. "Hi, Mama." I lay back down on my pillow and slept, a peaceful sleep. I had a renewed sense of acceptance and understanding. She was still here with us. It was just different now.

CHAPTER 49

Lucy

The days following my mother's death were a blur to me. A constant flow of people came and went from our home. Food delivered and served. Tears and laughter shared by many. My father and Julia kept busy with the arrangements while Kat and I took charge of greeting the many visitors who came to offer condolences. We tried keeping our younger siblings occupied and distracted. I gathered the many photographs we could find of our mother. Kaylan and Jessica helped me sort and organize the pictures into large poster-size collages. I had the girls and Mikey write letters to our mother. Sad, heart-wrenching feelings of loss and emotions scribbled down on paper.

Dear Mama...

You were the best mama. Please come back home. I'm sorry if I
misbehaved. I promise to be a better boy. I promise to listen to everything
you say. I miss you and love you. Please come back.

Love Mikey.

Mama,

I will miss you taking me to dance class. I will miss you picking us up
from school and making our beds. I will miss dinners with you and you
fixing my hair for church. My life will be so sad without you. I love you,
Mama.

Jessica

Mama,

Why did you leave us? Why did this happen? I'll never forget you. I will
think of you every minute of my life. I will never get over you. I'm sorry you
were sick. I'm sorry you can't be our mama anymore. I love you so much,
Mama.

Love, Kaylan

The wake was long and exhausting. So many people
came. A line of mourners wrapped the funeral home along the

outside porch and down the driveway. I stood in the appropriate spot among the receiving line as friends and relatives gave their condolences. I watched my father be brave and strong in one moment and then sad and weak the next.

My mother looked beautiful. Her face was no longer grey and stiff, but rosy and full again from the loads of makeup and the natural bloating of a decaying body. Her hair was colored and pretty again. She looked peaceful. Her body did, anyway.

I stood in the line and mechanically said thank you to many people. I thought about Jack. I allowed myself quiet moments here and there to think of him. I hadn't been able to speak with him since my mother died. He called once, but I wasn't home. I thought of his mother, about how Jack and Charles were torn apart after she died. How they were unable to mourn the loss together. How awful to not have the support of your family. I don't know how I would survive without my siblings in times like these. I felt sadness for them and for myself.

I looked around me and at all the chairs behind us where people sat and prayed with our family. Demetry was there, of course, and Amelia. That girl Sam was also there, in the crowd. I looked over at Kathryn and she seemed annoyed and irritated. *That Sam rubs her the wrong way,* I realized. I needed to talk to her about that.

The wake was a beautiful success, if there could be such a thing. In tribute to my mother, the amount of friends and family that came to support us was in direct relation to the kind of love and support they felt for my mother. Many loved her.

The funeral the next day was much of the same. My siblings and I prepared a letter of love and appreciation to our mother that Julia read in front of the church. We stood hand-in-hand as she spoke the words of our hearts during Mass. I watched the crowd as individuals wiped their tears from their faces. Her words were sorrowful and joyful, true and honest and beautiful.

I scanned the gathering of people and then I saw him. I stared for a long moment, not sure if what I was seeing was real. I thought I might pass out, standing up on the pulpit, in front of the church. My legs became weak and my emotions uncontrolled.

It was Jack. He was here. I wanted to run to him. I wanted to hang on him and cry. I wanted him to take away all my sadness, make everything better. Our eyes met and a shared sense of sadness was exchanged between us. My sister finished her speech and we proceeded to return to our pews for the remainder of the Mass. I sat quickly next to Kathryn and grabbed her hand. "They're here," I whispered.

"Who?"

"Jack and Charles. They're here!"

Kathryn turned in her seat to see if she could see them. They were too far back and there were too many people.

"Oh my gosh," Kathryn said as she looked forward at the priest. A slow smile spread across her face as she closed her eyes and said a prayer.

Jack and Charles disappeared after Mass and we didn't see them at the burial or the reception. Every time someone entered the room at the reception, my heart leapt and then collapsed from the disappointment of not seeing Jack. Kathryn stayed busy talking with relatives and sitting with my father whenever she could. My father had aged some. He was such a handsome, sweet man. I prayed that he would recover from this loss and find peace and happiness again.

Kathryn and I decided to stay at Demetry's that night after the funeral. We had relatives staying at our house and my father was more than relieved when we offered to sleep somewhere else. I looked forward to sitting at the small dining table in Demetry's little kitchen and feeling a sense of normal now that the services were over. My family could relax now, sit back and heal from the loss of our mother. Our lives could move forward, slowly but certainly. Kat and I decided that perhaps Jack and Charles went back to Charles' apartment to rest.

"I'm sure they drove all night and I know all too well how tiring that trip is," I said to Kat.

"They'll find us eventually."

We arrived at Demetry's house and somberly walked into the old familiar kitchen. Demetry was so sweet to Kat. He had snacks and drinks waiting and ready for us when we arrived. He approached me first and gave me a big, friendly hug.

"I'm really sorry, Lucy. I'm sorry for your family. You're such good people."

I looked up at Demetry and kissed him on his cheek. "Thank you, Demetry. You're a good friend to my sister. I really appreciate that."

"Oh, stop being so mushy, you two." Kat pulled me away from Demetry. Demetry didn't hesitate for one second and grabbed Kat into a strong embrace. She cried softly into Demetry's shirt. Demetry stood there, holding Kat tightly as she allowed herself to break down, releasing all of the day's stress and anxiety. I watched them, envious of their relationship. I decided I would give them some privacy and I walked into Kat's bedroom to take a shower.

I stepped into the bathtub and let the hot water fall across my face and my body. I closed my eyes and enjoyed the heat enveloping my hair and skin, rinsing away the tension as I bathed. I thought about Jack. A thrill of excitement flooded my body as I thought about how close he was. How he came for me. Soon, we would be together and I would feel his touch and see his face. I slowly washed my body with soap and let my hands move across my naked skin. I imagined Jack's hands moving across me, caressing my skin with his lips and his touch. I imagined Jack's body, so close to mine. My heart rate was pulsing as I thought about my life with Jack. What it could be like.

I slowly felt it all slip away. I felt the responsibility of my family come crashing down on me. My younger siblings, they needed me now more than ever. My father, he would need my help. I felt my thoughts take a sudden turn toward my current obligations, which are to take care of my family. Another realization was taking hold of me. Jack and I may never be.

I turned off the shower and got dressed, slowly pulling my comfortable sweats onto my legs, one inch at a time. I weakly opened Kat's dresser drawer and dragged out a T-shirt, grabbing the first thing that I saw, not interested in whether it was fashionable or not.

Kat was in the bedroom waiting for her turn in the bathroom. "What's wrong, Lucy? Are you okay?" she asked.

I looked at my sister now. She'd been removed from our family for some time. She'd never felt the strings of obligation when it came to our family. She'd never been overly concerned with my siblings and what they were doing. She'd been too free, too selfish in many ways.

"What do you think will happen now, with Dad, Kaylan, Jess, and Mikey? Who's going to take care of them?" I asked Kathryn, my voice cracking and tears flowing from my eyes.

"Oh Lucy. Don't cry about that now," Kat said comfortingly. "Dad will figure it out. We will all help him, Lucy, I promise you." Kathryn put her arm around me and kissed my face. "Let's try not to worry tonight. Let's try to take it easy on ourselves, okay Lucy?"

I smiled through my tears and silently nodded. Kathryn escaped into the bathroom to shower and I sat on her bed trying to compose myself.

I looked at myself in the mirror. My eyes were puffy and swollen, my hair damp and wet from the shower. I quickly combed it and pulled it up off my face. I sat defeated on the side of the bed with tissues in my hand, dabbing at my tears.

When will this end? When will I ever feel normal again? I placed my hands over my face and sat and cried quietly.

I heard a knock on the door. It must be Demetry. I stood and walked over to open the door. I blinked twice and then reached up and jumped into his arms.

It was Jack!

"Lucy, you poor thing. I'm here now," Jack said quietly as he rubbed my head gently.

"Jack, I can't believe it. I can't believe she's gone. I can't believe you're here," I sobbed into his neck.

"It's okay, let it all out," Jack said calmly. "I'm so sorry for you, Lucy. I'm so sorry about your mother. I loved your mother. She was a wonderful, caring person. So much like you, Lucy," Jack said as I cried into his arms. He pulled my face back off him so he could look into my eyes. He wiped my tears and bent down to kiss my lips.

"I missed you, incredibly," he whispered softly to me. I closed my eyes and listened to his voice as he spoke. He continued to kiss me gently on my face, the thrill of his touch echoing throughout my body. I couldn't think of anything but him.

"Jack, take me somewhere. I need to be with you," I pled as I kissed him urgently on his lips and whispered in his ear, "Please, Jack."

Jack stopped and looked down into my face, his caring, gentle eyes capturing mine. He turned and walked back into the kitchen where Charles was waiting for Kathryn. "Charles, do you mind if Lucy and I go back to your apartment?" Jack stared at his brother, silently begging him to not ask any questions. Charles looked up at us and tossed Jack the keys.

"Thank you, Charles," I said. "Please tell Kat not to worry about me. I'll be back tomorrow."

Charles stopped me quickly. "I'm very sorry, Lucy, about your mother."

"I appreciate that, Charles. Thank you both for traveling all this way to support us," I added. I looked up at Jack and we eagerly walked out of the house and into Pop's old pickup truck. Jack opened the door for me and helped me get in. He quickly ran around the truck and hopped into the driver seat. He stopped and pulled me closer to him on the bench seat so we were sitting side by side. He started the truck and drove down the road into town toward Charles' apartment.

I wrapped my arm around his and rested my head on his shoulder. "I can't believe you came," I said softly. "Is it weird to be back here, back in town?"

"My only concern is for you, Lucy. The few happy memories I have of this town are of you and your family."

I looked up at him and I felt years of sorrow for this man. Such a different life he had than I. Yet, somehow, we have suffered the same senseless loss of our mothers. Somehow, we have remained connected through our experiences.

Jack stopped his truck in front of Charles' building and got out to open my door. "I have to warn you, this isn't a great place," Jack said as I jumped out of the truck and into his arms.

I started to chuckle. "Yes, I know. I've been here before."

Jack and I turned and quickly walked down the sidewalk and into the building. He held my hand tightly as we jogged up the rundown stairwell to get into Charles' apartment. Jack took his keys out and opened the door, his hands visibly shaking. I walked in first as Jack quickly shut the door behind us and locked the deadbolt. I looked around the apartment. It looked exactly the same as the last time we were in it. The day we decided to search for Jack. The day it all began. I looked at Jack as he placed his keys on the table.

"This was where it all started, Jack. This was where we decided to find you, at all cost. Right here, in this apartment," I said as I walked around the living room.

Jack stood in the middle of the room, watching me intently. His expression told it all—his gratitude and his emotions written all over his face, his body language, his confidence and strength. His eyes, his face, are beautiful. I go to him. I want him badly. I want him to make me feel better. I need him to replace all my anxiety and depression. I need to feel love and affection.

He kissed me fiercely as tears escaped my eyes.

He stopped and gathered me and carried me into the bedroom. He laid me gently on the mattress and then proceeded to take his shirt off. I watched him undress. His body was strong and beautiful, his natural muscles perfectly formed. My body was shaking with anticipation. I sat up and knelt on the bed, removing my own shirt. I barely had it off and Jack was at my side, his pants unbuckled and hanging on his hips while he assisted me in removing my clothing. I looked down at his pants, embarrassed by my own insecurity and nakedness. Jack picked my chin up and met my uncertain eyes.

"You're beautiful, Lucy. Absolutely stunning."

I threw my arms around his neck and kissed him strongly. My heart was beating a million miles as I touched his chest and kissed his lips. My body felt desperate for his, desperate to have him inside me. I continued to undress, swiftly removing my pants. Jack did the same with a one-hand movement as he carefully lay on top of me. I wrapped my legs around his waist and held him tight. I could feel him through his boxers, so strong and stiff. He kissed me sweetly, his tongue gently probing and playing with mine. He pulled my hands up over my head and kissed my throat and chest. My body reached to touch his in every movement. His touch sending shivers straight down my body and between my legs. My thoughts were racing. *I love this man.*

How can I live without him?

Jack carefully removed my bra and gently caressed my breasts with his lips.

I think I might die without him.

I pulled him closer to me, rubbing him gently, eagerly.

"Lucy?" Jack stopped and looked into my face.

"Yes, Jack," I said breathlessly.

"I love you, Lucy. I've loved you for a long time. You mean everything to me." He talked delicately as he slowly removed my panties and quickly discarded his boxers. Small tears escaped my eyes as he readied himself to enter me. My arms locked tightly around his neck, his face inches from mine. His eyes, never leaving mine.

"I love you too, Jack. I love you too," I said desperately as he kissed me passionately and slowly entered my body.

I closed my eyes. My body reacted physically to his every move. His sweet caressing and gentle ways, his soft and affectionate touch building intensely in my body. "Oh god, Jack," I whispered. This man filled my soul with love, both physical and emotional. His rhythm grew deeper, and with it came feelings of pain and pleasure. My mind went blank, memories of my mother and the funeral long forgotten, each of us concentrating on fulfilling the other with all the lost love and emotions we'd secretly longed for, our bodies out of control, spasms overwhelming and blanketing our minds, grateful for the escape, grateful to be lost blissfully together as one.

Our bodies stilled, our limbs wrapped tightly around each other, neither one of us letting go, neither one of us escaping the other. Jack softly continued to kiss my face as I raked my fingernails gently down his back.

"I love you, Lucy," he said again as he rested his head on the pillow next to mine.

We drifted off to sleep, exhausted by our lives. Our bodies and minds, content and rested for the moment. I felt safe with his arms wrapped around my naked body. My soul had never felt so satisfied, so quieted. *I love this man. I need this man.*

CHAPTER 50

Lucy

Hours later, I woke alone in the bed. I quickly turned to look for Jack, and found him sitting in a chair by the window. He sat, his chest bare in his shabby jeans with his elbows on his knees and his hands on his face. I watched him quietly as he sat there in thought. I noticed his unshaven face, his rugged and strong-looking hands. I noticed the wave in his messy dark hair.

"Jack," I said, reaching out for him. He removed his hand from his face and held it out to me as he slowly came and knelt down next to me on the floor by the bed. "What's wrong?" I asked, my voice full of concern.

Jack rubbed my head and kissed my face and my lips softly. He smiled slowly as I closed my eyes to take in his attention. "I was just thinking about us," he said sadly.

I put my hand through his hair and looked at him, confused and baffled. "Why are you so upset?" I asked, nervous for his response.

"I can't move back here, Lucy. I can't leave my grandfather. I'm trying to figure out how this relationship will work for us."

I gathered the sheets around me and sat up in the bed. I pulled on Jack's arm and urged him to sit next to me. I took his hand into mine and slowly started to absorb the words that he was trying to say.

"I can't imagine what I will do without you. I feel so torn," Jack continued.

I sat and listened to him. I thought about my words carefully. I thought about my own family and my own responsibilities. I reached and turned Jack's face to look into mine. I kissed him and held his lips on mine for a long minute.

I whispered, "We don't have to figure this out tonight, Jack."

I know he's right. Our lives are complicated now.

"Can you come with me? Can you come to Indiana?" Jack asked with hope in his eyes.

I looked down at my hands. I thought how nice it would be to live on the farm, to be with Jack and his grandfather. I looked up at his face and shook my head no.

"I can't, Jack," I said softly. He looked away from me, disappointed. "My family needs me now," I said, my voice building up strength. I turned his face toward me and made him look in my eyes. "I love you, Jack. We have time. We have lots of time to figure this out."

Jack smiled at me, placed his hand on my cheek, and pulled me into a kiss. My heart began to race again. Why is this so complicated?

"You've saved me, Lucy. I will never get enough of you. I need you," Jack said as he slowly pulled the sheets down around my body. I threw my head back and allowed him to have full access to my neck and chest. He pulled me into his arms and held my naked body against his. We embraced each other, caressing each other's skin.

He made love to me. My mind and body will never be the same. My life forever changed by the single touch of this adoring, handsome man. I allowed myself the joy of the moment. I allowed myself the pleasure of our short and brief time together.

For now, it was enough. For now, I was grateful.

CHAPTER 51

Lucy

I walked Jack to his truck and watched him jump in and start her. He rolled down the window to say goodbye. An overwhelming sense of peace entered my soul. A ladybug landed on my nose and crawled quickly down my cheek.

Jack laughed. "She likes you," he said as he rubbed my other cheek with his finger. "Everything will be okay," he said sweetly.

I nodded my head yes and kissed him goodbye. I watched as he pulled away down the road. The ladybug reappeared and landed on my hand.

"Hey, Mama," I said as I slowly walked down the sidewalk.

THE END

Check author Susan B. Roara's Amazon author page

for the sequel to The Right Family

My Mother's Gift

coming soon

ABOUT THE AUTHOR

Susan B. Roara was born into a large family, which served as her inspiration for *The Right Family*. Today she is a mom of four and an entrepreneur, and writes in her free time. She's also the author of the forthcoming *My Mother's Gift*, the sequel to *The Right Family*.

The Right Family is her first book.

OCT - 2015

Made in the USA
Lexington, KY
27 October 2015